Caroline

Sarah Lamb

Paperback

ISBN: 979-8-9867275-0-9

For each woman who forges her own path through difficulties, you are amazing.

Also...

A special thank you to my Tuesday night accountability group. You've made me a better writer, and I appreciate your help as I stepped outside my genre and found I really enjoyed it.

Laura, thank you for tagging me. I'm forever grateful.

Hannah, for being my willing reader and cheerleader. You are an inspiration to me.

Chapter One

"Mrs. Hardy is looking for you," Mary the cook said as she walked in the kitchen with a tray.

"I wonder why," Caroline said, and looked up from the dishes she was washing. She dried her hands with a worn towel and took off her apron, draping it on the back of a chair. "I'd better go see. I'll finish those dishes when I get back."

As she made her way down the familiar twisting hallways of Mrs. Hardy's School for Girls, Caroline took a moment to reflect. She'd walked these hallways many times, left in the care of Mrs. Hardy by her father's lawyer at the age of twelve. As a girl, she attended classes here and made friends while learning advanced sums, Latin, French, and history. Hours were spent reading books and sewing. She'd had a good education, something her parents had insisted upon.

Once she had come of age, Mrs. Hardy offered to let her stay and gave room and board, along with a small salary, in exchange for helping where needed. Usually, that was in the kitchen. Other times, it was helping new students to prepare their rooms, and making sure that the girls were in bed at the required time. The days were long, the work tedious, but at least she had a roof over her head. Caroline couldn't complain. While growing up, Mrs. Hardy often told her how the world was harsh, even cruel to orphans. It was better to stay there with her, somewhere safe.

Pausing in front of a mirror, Caroline studied her appearance. Being called to Mrs. Hardy's office made her feel anxious. It always had. It wouldn't do to look disheveled. She was twenty-two, and ought to be as calm and poised as an adult, not disheveled like a child, yet that feeling of worry stuck in her throat.

She tugged on the collar of her work dress and straightened it. It was simple, but it was well made; Caroline had labored on it herself late at night, having discovered through childhood lessons that she was quite skilled with a needle. As a result, many of the mending tasks fell to her. It was also the only way she was able to have a new dress.

Nearby footsteps sounded, and swiftly, she smoothed her long, light brown hair and pulled away from the mirror. She didn't want anyone to think she was vain.

The laughter of young girls wafted down the hallway. Caroline smiled, then briskly walked toward Mrs. Hardy's study. She remembered being that age, and also laughing and joking with the girls she had gone to school with. Like the others, she had dreamed of a home of her own, a handsome husband, and a family she could raise.

However, unlike many of the other young women who had left the school, she did not have such a thing. That didn't mean she never would, Caroline reminded herself when she felt sad. It just meant it wasn't her time. Mrs. Hardy kept her busy, both during her time as a student and now as an employee. It didn't leave much time for meeting others and forming relationships.

Caroline tried to push her worries aside as she stood outside the study door. It was a dark wood, polished to gleaming, with a large brass knob. Caroline had polished it herself that very morning.

After a light knock, Caroline smoothed her dress again, took a deep breath, and tried to still the flutter in her stomach. Mrs. Hardy didn't usually ask anyone to come to her study. If something was needed, she came herself to the kitchen, or else sent one of the young ladies with a message. It was only when there was something serious that someone was told to see her.

What had she done? Caroline couldn't think what it might be. It had been at least two weeks since she'd burned anything in the kitchen or accidently scalded an apron while ironing.

"Come," a matronly voice called from behind the door.

Reluctantly, with her hand on the knob, Caroline slowly pushed the heavy, walnut door open and stepped into the room.

"Ah, Caroline. Close the door, please."

The flutter in her stomach grew, but Caroline obediently turned, closed the door, and then faced Mrs. Hardy again. "You wanted to see me, ma'am?" she asked.

Mrs. Hardy nodded. "Please, sit, dear." She pointed to one of the plush chairs in front of her desk, usually reserved for parents.

Dark curtains were open behind her, but the room was still dim. The oil lamp, freshly filled by Caroline herself that morning, shone brightly, but not enough to cut through the gloom.

Crossing the room, Caroline sat and folded her hands in her lap. There she waited quietly, observing the older woman.

In her late fifties, Mrs. Hardy was a woman with sharp eyes, a fast mind, and a quick tongue that would scold or praise at her whim. Caroline had seen her defuse many situations that could have been dire with parents over the years. She had also seen the headmistress, just moments from a student being withdrawn from her school, have the distraught parents suddenly offer a large and generous amount for their daughter to be allowed to stay. Mary once whispered that the older woman could sell a bald man a hairbrush, she was so persuasive.

Today, those steel-gray eyes were fixed on Caroline, with a predator's gaze that made her shiver. Caroline wasn't used to seeing that particular expression fixed on her.

Mrs. Hardy finally spoke. "You know, my dear Caroline, since you were twelve years old, an impressionable age for a young lady, you have been in my care. Since that early age, I have done all I can to teach you. You've learned what you need to become an accomplished young woman, and, dare I risk vanity by saying it, I think I have taught you well."

"Yes, ma'am," Caroline said, unsure where this was going. "You have, and I'm so grateful to you."

With a nod, Mrs. Hardy accepted the compliment. "You also know, your father's lawyer made me your guardian, a task which I quite readily accepted, and have strived diligently to fulfill."

Caroline lowered her head and nodded. Where was Mrs. Hardy going with this? Should she thank the woman again?

"And, as your guardian, I must do what is best for you. I allowed you to stay in my school, as you had no family and no prospects. Well, my dear. That is all about to change."

Curious, Caroline looked up to see the older woman's pleased expression. For some reason, it made her shiver, and she clasped her hands together. "What do you mean, Mrs. Hardy?" she asked.

"I mean," Mrs. Hardy said, then paused for a moment, turning up the oil lamp on her desk, "you are about to be married."

Chapter Two

"MARRIED?" MARY GASPED, HER teacup falling with a clatter and splashing on the table. "To who?"

"To her brother," Caroline said, tears rolling down her cheeks. Her throat was so tight it took all her effort to push the words out.

"That awful man?" Mary said, shock evident in her voice. She pushed a teacup with steaming chamomile tea toward Caroline and mopped up her own with a rag. "I've met him a few times," she muttered.

"Is he really that bad?" Caroline asked, distressed. "Mrs. Hardy seemed quite excited. She said we'd be family now. I wouldn't be alone anymore, and I'd be well off. Mrs. Hardy reminded me that she's always done what's best for me and to trust her." She twisted her dress between her fingers and gave a pleading look. "But I don't want to be married, not to someone I don't know. Someone I didn't choose. I don't even know what kind of person I want to marry."

With a frown, Mary nodded. "Not him. I'll tell you that. He is a disgusting man. He's older than Mrs. Hardy, you know. He plasters his nearly bald head with an oily tonic, which sometimes drips down his face. His breath reeks from the raw onions and garlic bulbs he eats. You can smell him from a room away."

"Evidently, he...he..." Caroline hiccupped, as she tried to contain her tears at Mary's description, "he is due for a large inheritance. But it's all dependent upon him being married."

"Well, of course it is," Mary muttered, nearly slamming her cup on the table. She threw up her hands. "And of course, she'd choose you. That woman has always had her own best interests at heart. You are so sweet and mild-mannered, you don't argue over anything. That makes you both the perfect ward and a future bride. I bet she gets something out of this we don't know about. What did you tell her?"

Caroline blinked. "What do you mean?"

"I mean, child, did you tell her you'd marry him?" Mary's tone was exasperated.

"I don't have a choice, Mary. She's my guardian. I have to do as she says," Caroline answered sadly and looked down into her teacup. "I am sure Mrs. Hardy is doing what she thinks is best for me."

"Sweet child, no, you don't have to marry him," Mary answered, softening her voice. "A guardian only makes decisions for you until you come of age. Do you mean to tell me you've been doing just what she told you to do these last few years?"

There was a long moment of silence. Then, Caroline spoke, her voice very small. "I did not know that. I always trusted Mrs. Hardy was looking out for me, like Papa and Mama said for her to. Do you really think that she's been using me?"

Mary sighed. "At least tell me you didn't sign anything. I know you, you are a smart girl. You wouldn't do something foolish like that, would you?"

Caroline hesitated, and her gaze fell.

"Oh, child! What will we do with you?"

"I didn't sign anything, not yet," Caroline assured, her chin raising quickly. Then, in a trembling voice asked, "Is he really that terrible? I don't want to get married yet, I don't, but Mrs. Hardy said that many girls marry, just for security, and convenience, and that..." her eyes widened. Her tone became hushed, full of horror. "Mary, if she lied to me all these years about the decisions she's made as my guardian, do you think she lied about this?"

Mary was quiet for a moment. "I think she lied simply for your money, child. Which she took. Every penny your dear parents had. As for this, I think it's the truth. To her, it's a marriage of convenience...it's convenient for her brother. Possibly even for her. Who knows what she will gain by it? I wouldn't be surprised if she's sold you to him."

"Sold me? Whatever shall I do? I don't want to marry him!" Caroline stood and paced in the small kitchen.

"I'm sure there's time to think about this and figure something out," Mary assured her. "When are you supposed to get married?"

"In three weeks," Caroline answered.

Mary pressed her lips together. She stood and walked over to a basket sitting near the front door. Inside was the previous day's newspaper, ready to be repurposed. She laid it on the workbench and opened it wide, looking for something. Caroline stood next to her, her stomach gnawing with anxiety.

"Did you see something that might help?" she asked, determined to stay calm, even though the thudding in her heart felt loud enough to drown out her words.

"Maybe," Mary muttered. "Hold on." Her finger moved against a column of nearly impossibly small text, then she stopped. "There. It's a coach schedule," she said as she tapped the page.

"A coach schedule?" Caroline repeated.

"Yes, of course. You've two choices, girl. Stay and be married, or go as far as your savings can take you. But whatever you do, don't tell me which you'll do. The less I know, the better it is for you."

Caroline bit her lower lip. Mary was right. Those were her only choices. Get married or leave. Both were frightening ideas. Each led her on a journey to the unknown. And the consequences...she didn't want to think about the consequences of either. A young woman married to a man like that, or a runaway girl without a job, without family...

She took a deep breath. "Mary, suppose I was to..." she lowered her voice, "leave. Suppose I did. How would I provide for my needs? I've never been on my own. I don't know what to do."

Mary nodded, understanding. "What you do, child, is look for a boarding house. One run by a respectable lady. Then, you look for work. You sew, offer yourself to take in small jobs. Or clean. Find a mother with too many babes and help her. Or a rich young'un that needs a teacher. Things aren't so bleak when you realize there are plenty of jobs you can do. And, you may not want to, but even a hotel might need a maid or a kitchen helper. You've experience in each of those things. It won't be a lie to tell them so."

Caroline closed her eyes and nodded. She took a deep breath and opened them. "You are right. I can do all of those things. Oh, I don't know what I'd do—what I'll do—without you and your advice."

With a laugh, Mary folded the newspaper and handed it to Caroline. "You'll do just fine. This isn't goodbye, I'm sure. Why, one day, I bet I'll get a letter from you, letting me know that you're as fine as the first flowers in spring. Perhaps even married to some tall handsome doctor."

With a laugh of her own, Caroline shook her head. "Oh no, not me." She hugged the older woman and tucked the newspaper into her apron pocket. "I've no intention of settling down any time soon. But I *will* write one day, when I feel it's safe to do so."

As the two released their hold, Caroline felt much lighter than she had just an hour before. Now there was only one thing to do, and that was to decide where she was going to go.

Chapter Three

MRS. HARDY NODDED A thank you as Caroline cleared her dessert plate from in front of her. She'd eaten, as had the girls attending the school, every bit of the beef stew, freshly baked bread with butter, and apple crumb cake. Caroline had enjoyed the meal herself, in the kitchen with Mary, Lizzie the maid, Jed the stable boy, and Don the driver.

Caroline remembered her days at the schoolgirl table. Back straight, only polite, low voices, no scraping of the utensils, and each bite of food a lesson in etiquette. She didn't miss those moments at all. In the kitchen, the four talked as friends, and with the occasional gossip thrown in, the conversation was never dull.

One thing she could say about Mrs. Hardy was she might be trying to marry her off to someone she'd never met, and who Mary was terrified of, but she really did know how to take a girl from any upbringing and turn her into a lady.

With the plates perfectly balanced in a stack, Caroline returned them to the kitchen and set them next to the basin of water. She pushed her sleeves up and grabbed the dish rag. Just as she plunged the first plate into the water, Mrs. Hardy walked in.

"Mary, would you leave us for a moment?" she asked.

"Of course, ma'am," Mary said, and left quickly.

Caroline bit her lip, shaking droplets from her hands and then drying them on the nearby rag. "Did you need me, Mrs. Hardy?" she asked as she turned around.

"Yes, I wished to speak with you for a moment," Mrs. Hardy said. "I've had wonderful news and thought you should know." Without pausing for Caroline's reaction, she continued. "My brother is arriving tomorrow evening. We've decided why wait? You'll be a bride the day after that."

"B-but..."

"Now, no need to worry. I'm sure you are concerned about a dress. Your lovely light blue spring gown will be fine. I'll loan you my best shawl, and I'll send the girls out to pick wildflowers for a bouquet. It will all be perfect, even if it feels a little rushed. Mary can make a small cake tomorrow, and it will be just lovely, you'll see."

Stepping toward Caroline, Mrs. Hardy put one hand on each of her arms and squeezed. The strength in her fingers belied the cheerful tone in her voice. "How lovely you'll look, my dear. A finer wife he couldn't hope for! So lovely. So obedient."

Her fingers squeezed tighter at the last word, sending shocks of pain in the soft flesh of Caroline's upper arms. It was sure to bruise.

Caroline tried to protest again. She squirmed a little as her skin grew tender and tears of pain formed. She gasped out, "Please. No. I don't want to." Mrs. Hardy's face turned cold.

"You will do as you are told," she hissed. "or you will face the consequences. I did not spend the last decade of my life caring for you, educating you, and giving you a chance for success to see you turn it down. You will do this. You have no choice."

Releasing her, Mrs. Hardy turned and left without another word or a look backward.

Her legs weak, Caroline slid to the floor. She felt betrayed, and the sudden realization that she was very much so alone was crushing. She wrapped her aching arms around herself, rubbing them.

Mary rushed in. "I heard the whole thing," she said grimly. She knelt and thrust a hand in her apron pocket, then pushed a small bundle into Caroline's hand. "It's not much. Just a few dollars. But it will help."

Caroline stared at the money; her mind was in such shock she could hardly register what the other woman was saying.

Mary continued, "You go pack, child. I'll bundle you a little food. In the morning, you'll go out to the market for me. But you won't come back. Do you understand what I'm telling you?"

With a nod, Caroline stood, and shakily pushed the money toward the older woman. "I can't. I shouldn't," she protested.

"Nonsense. Call it a loan if it makes you feel any better. It's not much, anyway. But it, and what you have, should get you a little way away. Maybe far enough to escape her."

Caroline nodded, and let Mary lead her numb body toward the door. "I'll finish the dishes," Mary said quietly. "Now go. Take only what you can that no one will see. As a matter of fact, pack it, and I'll stash it outside the kitchen. You can just pick it up on your way out tomorrow." She hugged Caroline tightly, and with a push, said, "Now, hurry."

As she left the kitchen, Caroline felt in a daze. How was it that things had happened so fast? When she got to the small room she'd called her own for the last ten years, she looked around. Though she didn't have much, she did have several things she loved. To choose what to take and what must stay would be difficult.

There was no choice though. Reaching under her bed, she pulled out a small bag. She packed her best dress, two others, and her hair brush, along with a few small trinkets. Then, she went to the loose floorboard in the back corner under her washstand and pulled it up enough to get to her small collection of money.

Counting it twice, she knotted it into a handkerchief and placed it in her small handbag. It wouldn't look suspicious carrying her purse when she went to the market for Mary, even if it was stuffed. Quickly, she'd looked around the room again. Was there room for anything else? What should she take?

She's just picked out the shawl to use when there was a knock at the door. Caroline froze, her chest tight with fear.

"It's just me," Mary's voice whispered.

Caroline opened the door and slid out her bag to the woman, who disappeared so swiftly it was as though she were an apparition.

Her life packed into a small bag, Caroline collapsed on her bed, closed her eyes, and prayed for strength for what was to come.

Chapter Four

THE ROOSTER ROAMING AROUND in the stable crowed its early morning call, waking Caroline up as it always did. She sat up, washed her face, and got dressed to help Mary start breakfast.

For a moment, she had forgotten. Then it all came back to her in a rush as she reached for her favorite dress and found the peg empty. Of course, she had packed it.

Donning another dress, she slipped on her stockings, then put a second pair over top. There. One more thing she didn't have to leave behind. She quickly gathered a few last trinkets into her handbag, grabbed a shawl, then wrapped a second overtop, and made her way downstairs. Caroline hoped that no one had discovered her hidden bag.

She dropped the newspaper, minus the stagecoach times, into the bin back by the kitchen door. Mary was there to greet her, her usually cheerful face one of concern.

"Caroline, I need you to go to the market," she said in a normal voice, in case anyone was nearby. "Don't you worry about helping with breakfast. Lizzie will help me. I've got to bake that cake, so I need you to leave right away."

She stopped, pulled Caroline into a fierce hug, and whispered in a choked voice, "I've put a little food into the market basket. Your bag is outside of the stable door. Hurry and go before the men finish with the animals and see you."

Caroline nodded. She wanted to say something. Thank you, perhaps. Or, I'll never forget you, but there was a lump in her throat, and she couldn't form the words.

Their eyes locked. Mary nodded, and Caroline realized she didn't have to say anything. Mary understood.

The older woman bustled her out the door, thrusting the basket at her. With a final squeeze of Mary's hand, Caroline turned and swiftly walked toward the barn, knowing Mary would return to her kitchen, preparing breakfast for Mrs. Hardy and the students as though it were quite a normal day.

Passing the barn, Caroline was relieved to find her bag stowed outside. Without pausing, she strode past and swooped it up, moving quickly with long strides to get as far away from the house as possible. The market basket was on her arm, and her mind worked frantically to form an excuse if anyone asked her where she was going, and why she was holding the luggage.

She glanced at it and noticed the broken leather buckle she'd always meant to have repaired. Yes, that was it. She was taking it to see if someone could repair the buckle. Was that believable? No, that wouldn't work. Surely one of the men at the school could have fixed it. Don, the driver, often fixed the leather reins. He'd have been able to do her strap.

With a sigh, she kept moving. She'd think of something else. With any luck, she wouldn't even need a story.

Caroline debated not walking along the dirt road on the short trip to town, but that might look suspicious and she feared missing the stagecoach, so instead, she kept the swift pace, and didn't turn to look over her shoulder until she was sure Mrs. Hardy's School for Girls was well out of sight.

It was only then she felt she could breathe slightly better.

As the town loomed ahead of her, Caroline paused to catch her breath. It wouldn't look good to be in a rush. Someone might think things were amiss. She continued on more slowly. Just ahead, Caroline could see the stagecoach. It wasn't loading yet, so she had time to get there before it departed. The real problem was how to get to it, without anyone seeing or stopping her.

A wagon drove past, a farmer in the seat. Sacks filled the back, along with two giggling children, who waved to her.

Caroline returned the gesture, slowing to let them get a little distance. Grit flew around in little swirls from the horse's hooves and the wagon's wheels, and Caroline felt it stick in her throat. With a cough, she raised her handkerchief to cover her nose.

She was closer now. Another hundred steps, perhaps, and she'd be at the station. Feeling for the small lump in her purse, Caroline wondered how far her meager savings would take her. She was determined not to spend any of Mary's money, unless she had no other choice.

Almost there. Caroline darted her eyes this way and that. Luckily, Hanson's General Store was right across from the station. It was easy enough to pretend that's where she was bound for, getting supplies for Mary or one of the girls at the school. However, so far, so good. She'd not seen—

"Caroline Watson! Yoohoo!"

Chapter Five

CAROLINE FROZE. SHE KNEW that voice. It was the one person she really was hoping not to run into. Mrs. Jenkins, the town gossip. With a smile plastered on her face, Caroline turned. "Good morning, Mrs. Jenkins," she answered politely, trying to slow the panic growing inside of her.

She clenched her bag, hoping the woman wouldn't ask about it. What would she say? She edged toward the general store.

"What are you doing so early?" the other woman asked, curiously.

"Mary sent me to get her a few things," Caroline answered with a smile, as she raised the basket. "She's making a cake this morning and most urgently needs to get her ingredients."

"And your luggage?" Mrs. Jenkins pressed.

Caroline forced herself to look down, as if she'd forgotten she was carrying it. "Oh, yes. I've a dress I'm hoping to find some complementary fabric for, to do over. I didn't want to get it dirty, so I carried it this way. You know how dusty the road can be. When was the last time we had rain?" Her heart fluttered a little as the lie slipped from her lips. Would Mrs. Jenkins question further?

Mrs. Jenkins nodded, "I recall you made that lilac dress of yours over last year. The lace you added at the throat and sleeves was quite pretty. Added a new skirt to it too, didn't you?"

Caroline forced herself to laugh. It allowed her to turn her head slightly, as she looked toward the station. They were hitching horses to the stagecoach. She didn't have much time. "Indeed," she answered. "I enjoy sewing. I'd love to chat more, but I'm afraid Mary made me promise to hurry back with her supplies."

"Of course. Don't keep her waiting, dear."

Relief flooded her, and Caroline smiled, "Do have a wonderful day, Mrs. Jenkins!"

The other woman nodded and turned, resuming the direction she'd been heading. Thankfully, opposite of where Caroline needed to go.

Rushing up to the station, Caroline found the stationmaster. "I need a ticket, please," she said breathlessly.

"We've three seats left," he told her, tugging at his beard. "You're lucky, miss, just about to leave. Where to?"

"Err, to, ah," Caroline froze. She couldn't ask how far her money would get her. That would be too obvious that she was running, but the fares hadn't been posted in the paper.

Just then, the driver came up. "You riding?" he asked. "I'll load your bag."

"Thank you," Caroline answered, and surrendered her bag. She still held the basket.

"Your destination, miss?" the stationmaster asked again. He tapped the chart. Next to it, an advertisement was tacked to the wall. It said, *Cottonwood Falls, Kansas. The place where dreams come true.*

Caroline looked at his finger. "Cottonwood Falls," she blurted.

The stationmaster pulled out a ticket and made a note. He said the price, and Caroline released a breath she didn't know she was holding. She had enough. And a little extra.

As she handed over the fare and took her ticket, she glanced at the other passengers who were lined up to enter. Luckily, she didn't know any of them. If anyone were to ask why she was traveling alone, she'd simply say she was a schoolteacher. It was expected they'd travel by themselves.

Feeling more confident, Caroline smiled, thanked the stationmaster, and joined the others waiting to be let into the stagecoach. The driver offered his hand, and with only a little difficulty Caroline climbed in.

With the market basket on her lap, she sat in the middle of two other women. Three men sat opposite. Caroline was grateful it wasn't a full coach. Four squeezed together on each side wouldn't have been pleasant; three was tight enough of a fit.

With a shout from the driver, the stagecoach lurched forward, and Caroline might have fallen from her seat had she not been wedged in. The horses' hooves thundered as they set off toward their destination.

One of the women pulled out a book and began to read. Each of the men held a newspaper. The other woman turned and gazed out the window. The oversized feather on her bonnet jiggled with the stagecoach's movement, tickling Caroline's face. Caroline tried to look out the window as well, but the view was blocked. She wished she had something to read, but contented herself with closing her eyes. Perhaps a short nap would make the journey pass sooner.

Somehow, Caroline fell asleep. She woke as the stagecoach slowed. "Rest ahead," the driver called in a loud voice.

Rubbing the sleep from her eyes, Caroline realized that her shoulders had become pillows for the female passengers on each side of her. They stirred, and she eagerly moved forward slightly, trying to get a little more room.

The rest stop was another station. The horses were switched, a few moments of comfort taken, and the stagecoach loaded again. To her surprise, only one woman got back in the coach, the other passengers stayed behind.

Caroline welcomed the extra room. She set her basket next to her. It was nearing lunchtime, but she was too nervous to eat. She'd peeked in the basket and saw Mary had put in several small loaves of bread, a few apples, and a good-sized wedge of cheese.

The woman across from her gave a sudden snarl, and Caroline jumped. When she realized the other woman was asleep and snoring, she relaxed and stared out the window.

There was too much to think about. Too much to worry about. It was overwhelming. What if Mrs. Hardy's brother found her? What if she couldn't find a place to stay or work to do when she got to Cottonwood Falls? What then?

Caroline refused to let tears form. There was no time for self-pity. Instead, she took a deep breath, sat as tall as she could, and focused on the future. Her future. For the first time, she'd be making her own decisions.

She only hoped it would be as simple as Mary acted.

Chapter Six

"Here we are, miss."

Caroline stepped out of the stagecoach, accepting the driver's hand.

"I'll get your bag," he stated, and climbed to the luggage rack on top of the stagecoach to unfasten her satchel.

Caroline took it from the driver and thanked him, then stepped onto the wooden sidewalk. Just as she turned for a look at the town, two children ran past. One bumped into her and she dropped her basket and stumbled backward. Her heels hung over the sidewalk and she frantically tried to catch her balance, her arms windmilling.

Strong arms wrapped around her waist, steadying her, and a polite voice asked, "Are you alright?" A scent of cloves mixed with soap enveloped her.

Her heart beating wildly, Caroline regained her footing and turned around to look at her rescuer. Standing a little taller than she was, he was dressed in a suit with a dark bowler hat. A small bag was on the ground next to him, reminding her of the kind her father used to carry.

In perhaps his early thirties, the man's face was clean shaven. As she ducked her head in embarrassment, she noticed his hands were strong looking, with long fingers and short nails impeccably groomed.

"Yes, thank you," she said, a faint blush forming at the closeness. "I am very grateful for your assistance, Mr…" she smiled and gave a small shrug.

The man removed his hat, revealing his dark blond hair, and gave a small nod. "Edward Mason, town doctor. Pleased to meet you."

"Caroline Watson," she replied softly. "Again, thank you."

The doctor flashed her a smile and said, "Well then, I'll be on my way, Miss Watson. A pleasant day to you."

"Wait!" Caroline called, reaching out to place her hand on his arm before she realized what she was doing. He looked down at her hand, blue eyes amused, and Caroline quickly pulled it away. "Do you…is there…" she tried to pull her thoughts together as his piercing eyes met hers, and her mind temporarily froze.

Caroline was surprised at herself. She'd never been one to lose her tongue, but talking to this man was different, for some reason.

She took a breath and tried again. "I apologize. It was a long journey. I'm looking for a place to stay for a while, so that I can find work."

Dr. Mason nodded and picked up his bag. "I can show you a pace to stay, perhaps," he offered. "Work, I'm not so sure about, but the landlady, she is mine as well, might have ideas on that. Follow me, it isn't far," he said, and stepped onto the sidewalk.

Grateful he didn't ask any personal questions, Caroline picked up her satchel and basket, and briskly followed. The doctor's long legs took him far, and she had to do one and a half steps for each of his. There wasn't much time to admire the town, but Caroline's eyes took in all they passed.

A typical town, there was a sundry store and a bar. The post office was in the stagecoach building, and a bakery and café took up a large section of a tall building.

Townsfolk walked in pairs, horses and wagons rode through the street, sending clouds of dust up. The sheriff leaned against the jail building, and over to one side, a little girl chased after a puppy.

Caroline looked around her in wonder. The town was much bigger than she'd imagined. Why, it was almost as though the long street of shops wouldn't end! There was a lumberyard, another general store, a hotel, and a blacksmith. Cottonwood Falls was a bustling place. Behind the rows of businesses, she saw town homes. Some with gardens, others close together. In the distance were more homes, more spread out. One had cattle, at another two small goats grazed.

When he saw she'd fallen a few steps behind, Dr. Mason slowed. "Large, isn't it?" he said. "When the Atchison, Topeka, and the Santa Fe built the rail line, the town boomed overnight. It's the perfect place to live if you want to be around a little bustle, but still have some elbow room."

Caroline caught up to him. "Is that why you are here?" she asked. "If you don't mind my asking. Your accent, it's northern. I wasn't expecting to hear that, here in Kansas."

The doctor stopped again. "That's what it is," he exclaimed. "You have one too. Michigan?"

"Why, yes," Caroline said. "I lived there until I was ten. Then, we moved to Kansas."

"I grew up there as well, and later went to the University of Michigan Medical School," the doctor said, and reached for her bag. "Let me help. It's not much farther." The two continued walking. "After medical school, I wanted to do more than just treat the wealthy, though the money is good. I traveled west, found a few small towns, stayed a while, but this one...this one I grew to love. It's not just the people or the scenery, it's...I'm not sure. But I felt like I needed to be here. I've been here almost two years now."

Caroline nodded. "Silly as it sounds, I felt the same when I saw the name on the coach schedule," she said.

The two rounded a corner and approached a large white house. A low white fence was in the front, protecting a vegetable garden. An older woman, her white hair tied back into a bun, was digging near a plant and looked up as they approached.

"Mrs. Meeks," the doctor called, "this young woman has just arrived in town and is looking for a place to stay." He set Caroline's bag down, turned to her, and with an apologetic expression, said, "I'm afraid I'm expected in town for an injury. I leave you in her capable hands." He tipped his hat and left, his long legs carrying him out of sight quickly back the way they had come.

Caroline stood watching him, then turned back to Mrs. Meeks, who was watching her with a small smile.

The other woman stood, brushed off her hands, and took Caroline's hand in her own as a greeting. "Welcome, my dear. Yes, I've just one room left for rent. The price includes your morning and evening meal. Would you like to see it?"

With a nod, Caroline answered. "I would. But I must be upfront, Mrs. Meeks. My circumstances are modest. I'm sure I have enough to cover a week's lodgings, perhaps two, but I am also seeking employment somewhere."

"That's no problem at all," Mrs. Meeks answered, and took Caroline's bag. "Perhaps I can help. What do you do?"

"Some of everything," Caroline said, as she followed the other woman through a side door leading into the kitchen.

Much like the kitchen at Mrs. Hardy's School for Girls, this one was large, bright, and with a scarred wooden workbench in the middle. Mrs. Meeks continued through to a hallway and then up the stairs.

"I've the kitchen down here, of course, and there's a sitting room for anyone to use. I keep a small office downstairs as well, and the dining room. That's where we take our meals. Upstairs I have my own room, Dr. Mason has a set of rooms, and there's one let to a traveling music teacher. He's not here right now, but pays me to hold his room. That leaves the one for you, if you'd like it. Each room has a lock on the inside of the door, and I expect it used at night, or when you are gone. You'll be given a key. I'm the only other person with a key for the lock."

She turned and gave Caroline a strict look. "I don't allow any men in the room," she warned.

Her cheeks hot, Caroline stuttered, "Of, of course not."

"Just like I don't allow women in any of the men's rooms," Mrs. Meeks continued, as if she'd not heard.

They passed two closed doors and Mrs. Meeks pulled a key from her belt. "Here you are, my dear. It's small, but adequate. Let's look and see if it would meet your needs."

After putting the key into the lock, Mrs. Meeks turned the handle and pushed the door open. As she stepped inside, Caroline followed.

The room was small, Mrs. Meeks was right, but it was no smaller than her room back at the school for girls. This one, however, had a large window overlooking a flower garden. Caroline gasped at the view. Flowers dotted the landscape with their bright colors, butterflies flitting on them, and birds rested on a bath.

"How beautiful," she said. "So peaceful looking. You are quite an expert in horticulture."

"I dabble," Mrs. Meeks said modestly.

Caroline studied the rest of the room. The bed was neatly made, with a blue and white quilt. There was a small washstand and basin, along with three small shelves placed on the wall. A large dresser sat in a corner, and a worn but comfortable looking chair sat in another corner.

"Would this do?" Mrs. Meeks asked.

"It's more than adequate," Caroline said, and bit her lip. She reached slowly for her purse and opened the clasp. "How much for the week?" she asked.

"Four dollars," Mrs. Meeks answered.

"Are you sure?" Caroline asked. "That seems rather...low."

"I think it's a fine rate, for a lovely girl like you."

Mrs. Meeks smiled and Caroline felt a rush of gratitude toward her. She nodded, loosened the knot on her handkerchief, and pulled the money out. "Here you are," she said. "Would it be possible to see the local paper if you have one? I'd like to look for a job as soon as possible."

"It's in the sitting room. Each week you'll find the newest copy there. It's for each of the boarders to read, so I ask that you not take it out of the room."

"Of course," Caroline murmured.

Mrs. Meeks gave her a quick look. "You've been traveling all day. I suspect you didn't even have breakfast."

"That's true," Caroline admitted.

"Lunch?" the older woman asked.

When Caroline shook her head, Mrs. Meeks said, "I thought not. Come, I was about to pour a cup of tea. Join me. I've some fresh baked bread and butter. We will have a piece and look at the newspaper together. I'm sure you'll find just what you are looking for here in Cottonwood Falls."

As Caroline followed the older woman down the stairs, she simply nodded. No one needed to know she wasn't looking for anything...she was running from it.

Chapter Seven

Caroline closed her door and walked downstairs. She'd slept better than she imagined that night. Even with her mind filled with worry over Mrs. Hardy, her brother, and how she would support herself, it seemed the moment dinner ended and she hit the soft pillow, she was asleep.

Now it was time to face her new life and find employment. She needed an income. What she had wouldn't last too long, even with Mrs. Meek's generosity in undercharging her for her room and meals.

The voice of Mrs. Meeks trickled out from the dining room, and Caroline walked in. The doctor was sitting, a plate loaded in front of him with biscuits, sausage, and grits. Mrs. Meeks was removing an empty plate and smiled when she saw her newest boarder.

"Good morning, dear. I hope you slept well." She gestured with her head to the table. "Help yourself to the food."

Caroline nodded and took a plate from a vacant table setting. "Good morning. Yes, I slept well, thank you."

Mrs. Meeks returned to her place at the table with a cup of tea and slid one toward Caroline. She turned to the doctor and asked, "Busy day?"

He nodded. "I expect so. I need to follow up on a broken arm, a newborn baby, stitches from a bar fight, and an infection that's not healing." He paused, and said, "Apologies, for such talk at the table."

"Oh, it doesn't bother me," Caroline smiled. "My father was a doctor. He would discuss his patients at the table often. Mama was actually his nurse."

Dr. Mason set his knife down and dabbed his chin. "How interesting. Where did he study?"

"Boston," Caroline said. "Then he finished in Michigan, which is where I was born. We moved from place to place while he served as a missionary doctor a few months out of the year."

"Boston, hm? I wonder if he knew Dr. Striber."

Mrs. Meeks interjected, "You know, Dr. Mason, you are so incredibly busy, and I'm sure that's just your morning load. Who knows what the afternoon will be."

The doctor nodded. "That's true," he said. Then, a wry smile twisted across his lips. "You sound like you are about to make a suggestion, Mrs. Meeks."

The older woman shrugged and took a slow sip of her tea. "Well, it just occurs to me that Miss Watson is acquainted with the medical field. Perhaps she could be of use to you. She was looking for a job, and even if she just helped tidy your office and kept your books, it might be beneficial for you both."

Caroline's cheeks colored. "Oh, Dr. Mason, I assure you, I wasn't asking—"

"Of course not," he agreed. "Mrs. Meeks is just determined to pair people up, in any capacity she deems beneficial for them, be it romance, leisure, or the workforce."

"Perhaps I do," Mrs. Meeks said, with a shrug, "but you could use a little help, Miss Watson could use a little income...isn't that a good match?"

"I am quite sure, madam, that in your mind it is so," Dr. Mason said to Mrs. Meeks. He turned his gaze toward Caroline. His sharp eyes looked at her critically.

She straightened her shoulders, prepared to argue that she'd be quite fine looking for a job somewhere, when he spoke again.

"I could use assistance," he said. "Perhaps it could come from you. Stop by my office this afternoon. I'll tell you what I need help with and the pay I can offer. You can see if it's something you'd be interested in." Dr. Mason stood and tossed his napkin on the table. "Another fine breakfast, Mrs. Meeks. I thank you."

Mrs. Meeks smiled and stood as the doctor did. Dr. Mason walked to a chair, picked up his medical case, and left. Mrs. Meeks closed the door behind him and returned to Caroline.

"You shouldn't have done that," Caroline said anxiously.

"And you shouldn't look so worried," Mrs. Meeks said. "Dr. Mason doesn't bite. He could use you, and you could use him." She studied Caroline carefully. "Perhaps in more ways than one."

"I don't know what you mean," Caroline said, clearing her throat. Her cheeks flushed in embarrassment and she hurriedly spooned blackberry jam on a biscuit and took a bite, avoiding eye contact. "This jam is amazing," she said, after she'd swallowed. "Just incredible."

Mrs. Meeks smiled proudly. "Thank you. I make my own jams. I seem to have a knack for putting things together and them turning out right."

Caroline tried to press her lips together to stop the laughter that wanted to bubble out. She liked the older woman, even if she seemed determined to push the doctor and Caroline together in some capacity. Who and what else had Mrs. Meeks matched in the town? She was curious to find out.

It was pointless though, in her case. Caroline had to blend in, to avoid drawing any attention to herself in order not to be discovered by Mrs. Hardy. She also wasn't interested in being married to someone she didn't know. That's why she ran away. Dr. Mason didn't appear to be interested in matrimony either, why else would he still be a bachelor? But perhaps this offer of employment would work out. She liked Mrs. Meeks. It would be nice to stay here for a while.

"...if you agree?"

Caroline looked up, surprised. She'd been lost in her thoughts and hadn't heard a word Mrs. Meeks had said.

"Oh...er," Caroline stammered, "I'm afraid..."

Mrs. Meeks smiled. "I was asking if you'd like me to show you around the town. I can point out the doctor's office for your call to him this afternoon, as well as all the other places you might be interested in."

"That would be lovely," Caroline said. "Right after I help you with the dishes."

It was Mrs. Meeks' turn to look surprised. "That's not necessary, dear. I do them myself."

"Nonsense," Caroline said. She rose, pushed up her sleeves, and gathered the plates. "I'm here, and I'm able to help today, so I will." She set off for the kitchen, glad to be doing something instead of sitting around and waiting to see the doctor this afternoon.

As she scrubbed the plates and listened to Mrs. Meeks chatter about the doctor, a strange feeling filled her that she couldn't quite place.

Caroline told herself the little flutter of excitement wasn't because she was seeing the doctor again. That tall handsome frame, the warm, friendly smile with a dry sense of humor she related to. No, the flutter wasn't for that, but because she was applying for a position. That was all.

But the thumping of her heart was trying to whisper something differently.

Chapter Eight

Mrs. Meeks picked up a basket by the front door and moved onto the front steps with Caroline. "I need to pick a few of these squash first to take to one of the general stores," she explained, as the two women set across the yard. "I'm just going to stop for a moment in there to drop them off. The owner, and my husband's old friend, dearly loves squash, but his wife's plants didn't survive."

"That's kind of you," Caroline said, as she helped cut the vegetables off the vine.

"Just being neighborly," the older woman said, standing and resting her hand on her back with a wince. "That's enough, dear," she said as the basket was nearly filled.

Wordlessly, Caroline took the basket and they walked through the fence. Mrs. Meeks tugged on the gate to make sure it latched and they set off down the street.

"This town is quite large," Caroline remarked. "I appreciate the wooden sidewalk you have. The street gets so muddy when horses travel through. I grew up in an area where the hem of my dress had to be dark, as I could never get the mud stains out."

"It is a good-sized town," Mrs. Meeks agreed. "Cottonwood Falls grew more once the train came. It makes its way through every few days. We even get some of our mail from it. Goes faster than the coach does."

"Do you get many passengers stopping?" Caroline asked.

"We do," the older woman said. "Trains don't go everywhere yet, though I hear one day they will. Can you imagine that? Some stop here to take the stagecoach. Others are merchants, selling fabric and buttons or pots or other catalog things. You know, knick-knacks or things too big to carry around as they sell them. They stay in the hotel for a few days and then move on."

Caroline's fingertips tingled at the word fabric. She wondered if she might be able to earn beyond her needs to purchase the material for a new dress. It had been so long since she'd had once, and wearing something new seemed a good symbol of starting a new life.

Mrs. Meeks began to point out the various shops as they drew closer. Caroline observed how even though the building fronts were tall and flat, each shop tried to have its own distinct feel, from either color, a rocking chair in front, a decorative sign, or a bit of greenery.

They passed a store with a large window and a muslin curtain covering the bottom half. A hitching post was in front, with two horses tied to it. They snickered as the women passed.

"That's the barber's place. He's good for minor injuries. He and Sam, the bartender, are good friends. The bar, not a place for a lady, mind you, is right over there." Mrs. Meeks gestured with her head.

Caroline glanced at the wide building. Though not even midday, she could tell it was filled with men. Piano music trickled out, along with loud laughter.

"We've a café. You might have seen it as you left the stagecoach platform. Jenny Martin runs that with her ma. Jenny's husband is a rancher. He's out on a cattle drive right now. Here, if you aren't traveling through or a shopkeeper, you are likely a farmer or a cattleman."

The women passed a man who tipped his hat.

"Sheriff Taylor," Mrs. Meeks said. "Good man. Keeps the town clean. That's the jail there. Shares a wall with the bank. Here is the general store I shop at the most. If he doesn't have it, he can likely order it." She paused, took the basket from Caroline, and said, "Let's drop this off, then I'll show you where the doctor works."

Caroline nodded. They walked into the store and were instantly greeted.

"Dorothy Meeks," a round-faced man called out. "Would those be some of your fine yellow squash I'm seeing?"

"They are indeed," Mrs. Meeks said, and she unloaded the vegetables on the counter in front of the man. "A gift for you, Jim. And an introduction. This here is Miss Caroline Watson. She's staying a while, looking for work. I'm hoping the doctor hires her. He could use a little help, he's so busy. Caroline, this is Jim Jefferies."

Jim nodded, "How do, miss. What brings you to these parts?"

Before Caroline could make an excuse, Mrs. Meeks answered for her. "Same as every other young person. Opportunity," she said, then asked, "Has my new pie tin come in yet?"

"Sorry, Dorothy," Jim answered. "Not yet. The train's delayed. Got robbed again."

Mrs. Meeks shook her head. "A shame decent folks can't ever travel without being bothered. It's alright, Jim. I'll stop by in a few days. Maybe then."

While the two talked, Caroline looked around the store. Her eye was drawn to rows of sweets in glass jars, a shelf of books she scanned the titles of, and a small selection of ribbon. She'd just walked to the fabric when Mrs. Meeks asked, "Are you ready, dear?"

"Yes," Caroline said, turning with a smile.

The two women left.

"I noticed you admiring the fabrics," Mrs. Meeks said, one outside. "Let me take you to Dan Brown's store. It has all the fabric you could ever want."

"I'd love that," Caroline said. "But do we have time?"

Mrs. Meeks frowned. "Perhaps not," she said. "Let me walk you to the doctor's office. I'll take you there another day."

Caroline nodded. She walked with Mrs. Meeks then paused as she saw the stagecoach unloading. A man got off, his eyes slowly looking around. A slightly crumpled hat perched on his head, and a rumpled dark suit stretched to cover his girth. Though she didn't know him, Caroline felt instantly concerned. The hairs on the back of her neck prickled.

"Here we are," Mrs. Meeks said.

"Thank you," Caroline said, forcing a smile. She turned to see if she was being watched, but the man was gone. "Well, wish me luck," she said, blowing out her nerves in a long breath.

"You don't need it," Mrs. Meeks told her, and gave a wink. "I'll see you back at the house later."

Caroline squeezed her handbag a little tighter, took a deep breath, and pushed open the door.

Chapter Nine

THE DOCTOR'S OFFICE WAS small, a nook really, tucked between a tailor and the bank. The first thing Caroline noticed when she pushed open the door was a faint smell of disinfectant. She nodded in approval.

It was curious to her that so many doctors saw no value in washing their hands or their instruments before treating patients. Her father had often extolled the virtues of being clean, if at all possible, when treating a patient.

"It reduces the likelihood of infections," she remembered him arguing one evening at dinner to another doctor who had called it a waste of time and resources when treating poorer patients.

A small smile formed as she remembered her parents. How she missed them. It made these memories all the more special to her.

Walking inside the rest of the way, Caroline called out quietly, "Hello? Dr. Mason?"

A door in the rear of the room opened, and the doctor strode out. "Miss Watson," he said. "Welcome to my office."

"It's quite orderly," Caroline said, nodding her approval.

"For now. But only because I spend what feels like half the night here to get it that way for the next morning. To have someone helping would allow me more time to focus on the other things I need to do."

"And perhaps rest," Caroline said wryly, as she glimpsed the hint of shadow under his eyes.

The doctor gave his own slightly sarcastic smile. "Perhaps," he said. He gestured, "Let me show you around, explain what I need, and see if you are interested."

Caroline nodded and followed him around the office.

"This is the main room," he explained. "My financial ledger is here, and it's behind. I also need someone to rewrite my patient notes in this journal here. I keep two sets, a report on each patient who visits me, and then another set for myself, as a whole, to refer back to if there might be a similar case, especially one that was unusual," he explained.

"That's quite organized," Caroline said.

"We might be on the frontier, but there can still be civilization," Dr. Mason said. "Good records lead to good results."

"I agree," Caroline answered as she peered at the books. The doctor moved, forcing her to move with him. She wanted to ask more questions, but also didn't want to risk losing the opportunity to work for him by talking too much.

He gestured to a few chairs. "Sometimes someone will come with the patient, and I need privacy with them, or space. That's what these chairs are for. I try to keep this front room clean. Follow me to the examination room," he said. "That's where I keep my instruments, which I also sterilize. Sometimes I need assistance with that."

Caroline followed closely. As they went through the door, she stopped and grabbed on to the doorframe for support. Memories flooded over her, and for a moment, she could see her parents in a similar room, talking about patients as they worked together to sterilize the equipment they'd used that afternoon. Young Caroline watched from the door while practicing tying bandages on her doll's leg.

Dr. Mason looked over his shoulder. "Are you well?" he asked, seeing her hesitation. "Do the sight of instruments make you feel uncomfortable?"

Caroline shook her head. "I'm quite well. It just brings back memories of going into my father's office as a girl. Nostalgia." She made a sweeping motion to encompass the room. "This is also so clean. I applaud you for that. Your patients are fortunate to be treated by a man who believes in keeping his office and his tools clean."

"It reduces the likelihood of infections," he said, echoing the words she'd recalled just moments before.

"Indeed," Caroline agreed. "That is how I was raised." She glanced around the room and saw two baskets and a closed hamper. "Who does your linens?" she asked, motioning to the long strips of cloth that filled one of the baskets.

"A woman who lives outside of town. She washes for me once a week. Sheets and bandages. I usually have a good supply of the bandages on hand. However, she doesn't roll them when she returns them."

"That's something I can do," Caroline assured him. She reached for one of the clean bandage strips at the same moment he did.

Their fingers brushed, and tingles shot through her hand to her stomach. Startled, she looked up and found herself drawn into his hazel eyes, the doctor's head alarmingly close to her own.

Chapter Ten

CAROLINE BLINKED, AND TIME seemed to slow. The two were so close, she could feel his warm breath caressing her cheek.

Suddenly, clearing his throat, the doctor rose. "Well," he said, thrusting his hands in his pockets, "that's what I'm needing. Help to stay on top of things."

Her fingers deftly rolling the bandage, Caroline set it down in a small basket of already rolled cloth. "That I can do easily," she said. "And whatever else you might need, perhaps I can also assist with."

The doctor paused, then nodded slowly. "Yes, you know, at times, I do need an extra pair of hands. I will remember your offer, Miss Watson."

"Caroline is fine," she stammered, and grabbed for another bandage to cover her sudden embarrassment.

"Caroline then," he said with an amused smile. He reached over and took the rolled bandage from her. Their fingers brushed again. "Then you must call me Edward."

Her eyes raised toward his, and her stomach exploded into butterflies. Pushing down the feeling, she smiled neutrally and nodded. "Edward, then," she said, much the same as he had. "When would you like me to start?"

"Today, if possible," he said. "It's been a devil—excuse me. It's been a long day, and it's only just after midday." He scrubbed his face with his hand and sighed.

"Of course," Caroline said. "I'll start with your notes and ledger first?"

A look of relief flashed over his face. "That would be wonderful. But I must address the unsaid. I'm afraid I cannot pay you much. My office is given to me by the town. My own fees, though I try to collect them, are often paid in the form of chickens, or vegetables. Your pay might vary by week," he said apologetically.

"Then that's what it will do," Caroline said with a small shrug. "If I must, I'm handy with a needle, and perhaps I can pick up a little work on the side. As long as I have enough to pay for my room, perhaps a little more, I shall be quite content."

"You are rare," Edward said, and shook his head in wonder. "Really, you are."

She didn't know why, but his words made her heart feel light. Caroline smiled at the warmth filling her.

"I'm just myself," she said with a smile, then crossed into the outer room, picked up the pencil laying on his small desk and sat herself down, opening the first book. Within moments, she was deeply absorbed in the doctor's notes, neatly copying them.

From the corner of her eye, she saw Edward watch her for a moment, then returned to his exam room, and the rolling of bandages.

* * *

She wasn't sure how much time had passed, but enough had that her hand was feeling cramped. As Caroline shook it to improve her blood circulation, the doctor stepped into the room.

"Ready for supper?" he asked. "Mrs. Meeks puts up a fine meal. When I don't have to miss it, I don't like to."

"Oh, yes," Caroline said. "Would you like me to continue working on these after dinner?" she gestured to the stack of notes.

Edward shook his head. "No, tomorrow is soon enough. They've sat for a week now."

With a quick nod, Caroline stood and smoothed her dress. Edward reached past her and picked up a basket that was tucked in a corner. She looked at it curiously.

"Rent," he joked, hefting the contents.

Caroline laughed and peeked at it. An assortment of potatoes, carrots, and a cloth wrapped object lay in the basket.

"I knew you weren't joking," she said as they stepped outside. "Papa was sometimes paid that way too. But does it ever bother you that if you were back in the north, you'd be paid a doctor's proper wages?"

Edward looked thoughtful as he slowed his long strides to match her shorter ones. "Never once," he finally said. "That's why these people need me so much. Their first few doctors wouldn't work for barter. It was coin or no care. A good number of illnesses were left untreated. Bones weren't set properly, children died. These folks did the best they could on their own, but there are some things modern medicine and proper training can make a difference on."

"I understand the barber did a few medical treatments," Caroline said.

Edward winced. "He did. He does. And that's all they had, between times. But sometimes, that's not enough. He's a good man, and he's done many good things," he paused to tip his hat to an elderly woman who waved and "yoohoo'd" across the street, "but there's no substitute for a doctor."

"You are a selfless being," Caroline said, as they stepped off the sidewalk. Mrs. Meek's house rose ahead.

"Not entirely," Edward answered. His voice was dry as he answered. "I enjoy the freedom to be myself. To practice the way I see will serve these people best." Then, his tone grew curious.

"Tell me, Caroline. What brings you here?"

Chapter Eleven

CAROLINE'S MOUTH GREW DRY. Her step faltered, and the words in her mouth seemed to stick. From the corner of her eye, she saw the doctor was looking at her. What should she say? If she told the truth, that might be dangerous. He wouldn't want to let her work for him if he thought she was in trouble or a runaway. Towns didn't like troublemakers, and would drive them out.

Her mind spun frantically with thoughts. She didn't want to lie. Once you started to lie, it was much too hard to keep up with the story. The truth was always best, but...how much of the truth?

"I'm an orphan," she said, finally. "Since I was twelve. So, of course, I need a way to support myself. With the railroad coming through here, like others, I thought it might be a place of opportunity."

"It is indeed," Edward said. "Though, I am sorry. I wasn't trying to pry."

"It's fine," Caroline said and shrugged at him.

"Did you live with family, then? After your parent's deaths?"

"No, unfortunately I don't have any extended family. I lived with a family friend who ran a school for girls. She was given guardianship of me. I stayed with her until I was of age, and just past, but I wanted to do more than just help in her kitchen."

Edward nodded and opened the latch on Mrs. Meek's fence gate. "I understand. That's not a very interesting job, nor one that stimulates the mind. That's why I like medicine."

"Me too," Caroline said. "My father was a brilliant doctor. He was kind and patient, but so smart."

"Have you considered studying medicine yourself?" Edward asked. "Just recently, the University of Michigan has allowed women to study there."

"I've never really thought about it," Caroline said thoughtfully. Was that something she might want to do?

The two walked up the front stairs, and Edward paused, his hand on the door knob. "Never?"

"I'd always hoped to learn more from Papa," Caroline finished, her voice becoming sad. "It was not to be though."

"I'm sorry you didn't have the chance, but please, ask me any questions you have. I'll share what I know," Edward promised.

Caroline raised her eyes to meet his. His offer seemed sincere. The doctor's dark eyes were piercing with earnestness, and the fluttering in her stomach returned.

"Thank you," she said softly. "I am very grateful to you. For that, and for the offer of the job."

"If I can ever do more, please ask," he answered, his eyes not leaving hers.

Edward was about to say something else when the front door opened. Mrs. Meeks smiled at the two and exclaimed, "There you are! It's time for the evening meal. Come in!"

"I've brought part of my rent payment," Edward said, holding up the basket.

"And another part was dropped off by Jesse Stevenson," Mrs. Meeks said. "It's a strawberry pie!"

"Let me just wash, and I'll be right there," Edward said, handing over the basket.

"I'll do the same," Caroline said. "And let me know how I can help you, Mrs. Meeks."

"It's all done, dear. Just meet me at the table," the older woman said with a wink.

Caroline escaped to her room and poured some water into the stand basin. She splashed some on her face, cooling her cheeks. There was something about talking to the doctor that made her feel warm all over.

It was his kindness, nothing more, she told herself firmly. But yet...what if it was more than that? Was this what it felt like to be interested in someone? Could she let herself, even if only for a moment, dare to think of him as being more than just polite? As showing a personal interest in her? She really didn't know.

Caroline shook her head, then dried her face with a clean but worn towel. No. It couldn't be anything more. She was a woman with secrets. Someone as good as the doctor didn't need to be burdened with her past. Even being friends might be dangerous. Still, it would be nice to have someone to talk to. To laugh with, and share a common passion, medicine.

The subject had always fascinated her, and being in his office reminded Caroline of that desire to both help others and work in such an interesting field. It was much more enjoyable than anything else she could think of.

With a small sigh, she smoothed her hair and went downstairs. The doctor and Mrs. Meeks were sitting down. She took her spot as well. They said grace, then Mrs. Meeks passed around a large bowl of mashed potatoes, another of freshly picked green beans, some cornbread, and roasted chicken.

"Eat up, eat up," Mrs. Meeks clucked, when Caroline took modest portions.

"Mrs. Meeks," Edward said, as he slathered butter on a piece of cornbread, "did your day go well?"

"It did, Doctor," the older woman answered. "What of yours? Were you able to help Dan Thompson with his broken leg?"

The doctor grimaced. "If he doesn't stay off it, he's not going to have a leg. It's not going to heal."

Mrs. Meeks shook her head. "A stubborn one he is. Caroline, dear, did you enjoy your time at the office?"

"I did," Caroline answered. "I've started copying the doctor's patient notes. I'm looking forward to continuing tomorrow. Some are fascinating to read."

"I'm thrilled you suggested Caroline. Her help will be invaluable," Edward said as he nodded to Mrs. Meeks.

"How wonderful!" Mrs. Meeks exclaimed. "I knew you'd be perfect together!"

While the older woman clapped her hands once in an excited gesture, Caroline and Edward met each other's eyes, then quickly looked away again.

The rest of dinner's conversation was light. Afterward, Caroline helped with the dishes despite Mrs. Meek's objections. Just as she was climbing the stairs for the night, she glanced out of the window and saw a man walking slowly past the house.

It was the same one from the stagecoach station. She recognized the hat, the stretched too tightly suit. Involuntarily, Caroline's stomach clenched, and her breathing grew tight.

Who was that man? Was he looking for her?

Chapter Twelve

CAROLINE STRETCHED, PLACING HER hands on her lower back as she arched backward. She shrugged her shoulders to ease the ache and looked at the ledger in front of her.

She had been trying to work on the doctor's bookkeeping, and it was obvious that it wasn't something he did very much of. To say it was a mess was an understatement.

There was a loud thud outside followed by some shouts. Caroline looked toward the window in concern, just as the door burst open.

Several men ran inside, one groaning, his hand wrapped in a dirty rag.

"Where's the doc?" the shopkeeper, Jim Jefferies, shouted.

"I'm here," the doctor called, pushing his way through the doorway behind the men. "I was on my way back when a boy came and got me." Edward's hair was ruffled, and he was panting. It was obvious he had been running.

He turned to the crowd. "I need room. Stay back, please. Caroline, lay out my instruments, bandages, and wound supplies. I'll need you to assist," he ordered.

Caroline immediately grabbed his satchel and ran into the other room. As she pulled the instruments out of the bag, she cleaned each, then laid them on a small cloth-covered table where just an hour before, she'd put a fresh linen.

Several folded linen scraps followed, along with rolled bandages in different sizes.

"Rolled right over his hand," a man was saying.

"Crushed it," Jim said. "Got him here as fast as we could."

"I'll take a look," Edward said, his voice growing louder as he moved closer to his exam room. "Come, Mr. Dunfree."

Two men helped Mr. Dunfree into the room. Caroline pressed back against the wall to give them space in the tiny room to help the man on the examination table.

Mr. Dunfree's forehead was covered in sweat. Wispy strands of gray hair clung to the moisture, and he groaned and clutched his hand. "The pain," he groaned. "Hurts."

"Caroline," Edward started. "I'll need—"

"It's right here," she offered, holding the laudanum bottle, where a small dose had been freshly poured into a tiny cup.

"Thank you," he said as he held it to the man's lips. "Drink. I need to see your hand."

Caroline fetched a small basin of clean water and brought it near the instruments as the doctor examined the roughly bandaged hand.

"Hold still," he ordered as the wounded man tried to pull back his arm.

With a grunt, Mr. Dunfree laid back on the table.

"I'll prop his arm," Caroline said, and gently wedged a small bundle of cloth under his elbow. This elevated his hand slightly.

"Good," the doctor said. He quickly cleaned his hands by pouring alcohol over them and rubbing them together. Carefully, he unrolled the bandage wrapped around the crushed hand.

Mr. Dunfree's hand was mangled. His fingers were crooked, raw, and oozing, but the doctor didn't flinch. Caroline didn't either, though she had a feeling what would have to happen.

"I'm not sure I can save your hand," Edward warned, his tone as calm as if he were discussing the weather. "But I will save as much as I can."

From the doorway, Jim spoke. Caroline startled. She'd forgotten he was there.

"Do what you need, Doc. Thumb looks the worst."

"It does," agreed the doctor. "After it's cleaned, I'll know better. Perhaps I can save most of his fingers."

He turned to Caroline. "I need to find a book. Can you clean his hand?"

Caroline nodded and immediately reached for the basin and a soft cloth. Talking quietly to the injured man, she dabbed at his fingers, washing the blood away. His wound was severe. She wasn't sure how the doctor would be able to save the man's hand, but she prayed he could. Accidents were a way of life, but made it difficult to work with only one hand.

The doctor and Jim were talking in the next room, but she couldn't really hear them. A few moments later, they reentered, Jim leaning back against the doorframe.

"Well done," Edward praised as he looked at the cleaned wound. He examined the hand once more, pressing the fingers and manipulating each. Occasionally, he'd glance at his book with a frown or a thoughtful look.

Caroline looked at the page too. It was a diagram of the hand, showing the position of each bone.

With grim determination etched across his face, the doctor got to work. "Jim, Caroline," he said. "Hold him down."

Chapter Thirteen

As SHE GATHERED THE pile of bloody cloth and rags and set them aside to be cleaned, Caroline marveled at the last two hours. She was exhausted, yet the doctor had barely even seemed to sweat. His concentration had not once wavered, nor had he paused for a moment, except to look closely at the book's hand diagram.

The doctor was in the other room now with Mr. and Mrs. Dunfrees and Jim, giving aftercare procedures to them.

She wiped out the empty basin, then wiped it again, this time with disinfectant. Placing it back in its proper position, she set to work on the instruments, laid out upon the now stained cloth.

The outer door opened, then closed, and Edward walked into the exam room.

"You were wonderful," he said, without any pretense. "I've hardly worked with you, and I already know I don't want to be without you."

Her head lowered over the instruments as she cleaned, Caroline flushed with pleasure. That was the first time anyone had said such a thing to her. It made her feel special, desired. Her fingers froze over the scalpel she was cleaning.

Desired? Where had that word come from? He was simply talking about her medical skill. Nothing more. But was there more to his words? She barely managed to answer. "I'm glad I was able to assist," she said, proud she didn't stumble over the words.

"You did more than that," Edward said. He picked up his book, studied it a moment and closed it, walking out to return it to his shelf. "Somehow, you anticipated what I would need and had it ready for me before I even asked."

"That was simply experience," Caroline smiled. "Remember, I assisted my father many times. I have a good memory."

"At such a young age?" Edward asked, surprised. "I did not realize you also helped with operations."

"I had to," she shrugged. "For a time, Papa traveled the frontier as a missionary doctor. Like you, he wanted to help those who were at a disadvantage, so, three months out of the year, we left our home and traveled. Mama, as I'd said, was his nurse, and I...well, I suppose I just did what was needed. There were times extra hands were needed, and if Mama wasn't available, or if she wasn't enough to help in that situation, I'd assist. There were many times it took all three of us to help a patient."

"Astounding," he said.

Caroline inspected the cleaned instruments and returned them to the doctor's bag while the doctor wiped down the surgery table.

"What's astounding is that you were able to save Mr. Dunfree's hand," she said. "Every single finger." She shook her head in wonder, admiration coloring her words.

"I hope I did," Edward said. He ran a hand through his hair and sighed. "Time will tell."

"I feel sure of it," Caroline replied. Before she realized what she was doing, she laid her hand on his arm. "You've an incredible skill. These people are lucky to have you."

Edward looked at her hand, and as Caroline started to move it, he captured it in his own.

Her heart sounded as loudly as the blacksmith's hammer at his anvil. His hands were warm, a little rough from frequent use and washing, and the faint smell of cloves and disinfectant tickled her nose. Her mind swirled with the sensations, and she felt lightheaded.

"Caroline," Edward said, but he was interrupted. The outer door opened again and he released her hand.

The two turned toward the office room. "I'll finish here," Edward said, "if you don't mind seeing who that is?"

Caroline nodded and went out to where a child was waiting. "Hello," she greeted her.

"My ma wants me to give this to the doc," the little girl said, holding up a small sack.

"Thank you," Caroline said, as she took it.

Without another word, the girl left. Caroline turned back to the exam room. "This is for you," she said, offering the bundle.

Edward gave wince when he saw it. "Put it in with the linens to be laundered," he sighed. "I treated her mother for a post childbirth complication and left some clean linen there, since they had none. I'm glad it was returned, but it must be well sanitized before we use it again."

Caroline nodded and tossed it with the other items to be laundered in a large basket. "It's good the linens will be cleaned tomorrow. We amassed quite a collection of dirties today."

"I agree. On my way home I'll visit the washer woman to let her know to be sure not to skip us tomorrow. Now, I've got to make a few visits," he said, picking up his bag that Caroline had repacked. "But I hope I'll be back in time to walk you home."

With a warm smile, he left.

Staring at the closed door, Caroline couldn't stop the smile from forming. Somehow, without her even knowing when it happened, she'd found herself more than enjoying the doctor's company. It appeared that he felt the same. Now, if only she knew what to do next.

Chapter Fourteen

SEVERAL WEEKS HAD PASSED, and in that time Caroline had found herself almost feeling at home, in Cottonwood Falls. Each morning, Mrs. Meeks served a large breakfast. Quite often, several leftover pieces made their way into a small basket for Caroline and the doctor to take to the office.

The days were spent helping patients, working on correcting the bookkeeping, copying notes, and when there was a little time where things felt almost caught up, enjoying each other's company.

Caroline noticed the doctor rarely socialized. He was polite to his patients, but he wasn't overly friendly or on a first name basis with more than a few. He didn't visit the bar or play cards, though he'd nod along at the stories others told him of their card games. She had wondered about that, as he'd lived there for a few years. When she asked, he explained it was simply that he didn't allow himself to get too attached to the local people.

Edward explained that many were as transient as he had been at one time. It was too complicated to get to know someone, simply for them to move on a few weeks later. In addition, most of the people who lived on the outskirts of town were also distrustful of doctors, as in the case of the woman's daughter who had returned the soiled linen, so a slight distance was needed. There were only a few he called by first name, and those were the ones who had been there longer than him and established, like the shopkeeper.

Caroline figured he'd expected the same from her, a short stay there in Cottonwood Falls before moving on, and planned to prove him wrong. Now that she'd found her place, she intended to keep it and get to know everyone better.

She dressed, reaching for her rose-colored dress. Mrs. Meeks had taken her yesterday into the fabric shop, where she'd picked out some inexpensive, but pretty, material with plans to make a new dress. She hoped once it was done, she'd also be able to get a few small sewing jobs from the townsfolk. Those could easily be worked on in the evenings while her days were spent with the doctor, and allow her to make good on her intention to reimburse Mary for the money she'd given her to escape.

As she went down the stairs, Mrs. Meeks greeted her with a cheery good morning. "The doctor has already left," she explained, as she began to heap Caroline's place with breakfast. "Someone had an emergency. He said to tell you he'll meet you at the office when he's done."

Caroline nodded. "Thank you," she said. "Also, in case I'd not said it before, thank you for helping me to get that job. I truly enjoy working for the doctor."

"He's quite handsome too," Mrs. Meeks said, in a knowing tone.

"Well, that is, I mean," Caroline's words seemed stuck in her throat.

Mrs. Meeks laughed. "Don't worry, dear. I'm not trying to embarrass you. I'm just saying that you and the doctor would make a fine pair."

Caroline's face grew troubled. "I'm afraid not," she said. "I admit, it would be wonderful to think that, perhaps one day, but," she paused, not sure what she should say. Her secret was starting to get heavy to carry.

She'd never known what a burden it would be to hide such a large part of herself from others. There was the constant fear that once they knew she had run away from her guardian they'd distain her, or be fearful for their safety as she helped in the doctor's office if they thought it was because she was irresponsible. Caroline didn't want to have the reputation of a troublemaker. She valued the friendship of Mrs. Meeks and the doctor too much for that.

"Something is bothering you," Mrs. Meeks said kindly. "I've known it since you came. You've left something, dear, and you are worried it will find you."

Desperation in her voice at the woman's understanding, Caroline blurted, "I promise, Mrs. Meeks, I'd never be here if I thought it might hurt you in any way."

Mrs. Meeks nodded. "I know. I'm a good judge of character." She pushed a cup of tea toward Caroline, then took a slow sip from her own. "Do you want to tell me about it? Perhaps I can help."

Caroline's fork made trails through the steaming grits. Little rivers of butter swam in them. Did she want to tell Mrs. Meeks? She felt she could trust the woman, and...perhaps it would be nice to have her help. She'd not seen the strange man for almost a week, and maybe he had not even been looking for her, but that didn't mean anything. She had the feeling Mrs. Hardy wouldn't give up until she was back and married to her brother. Like Mary said, she wouldn't want her pride wounded.

Most worrying was not that idea, but what they might do to her once they found her, for delaying their plans. The memory of Mrs. Hardy bruising her arms, the flash of anger in her face, the hissing of her words stayed firmly in the forefront of Caroline's mind.

"I think I would like to tell you," Caroline said, taking a deep breath and setting her fork down.

Mrs. Meeks nodded.

Caroline waited a moment, ignoring the feeling of apprehension that tried to rise in her, then said, "You know I'm an orphan. And what I told the doctor when I first came is true. I was given as a ward to a woman who ran a girl's school. She was friends with my parents. I stayed there a while after I was of age, as I had nowhere else to go. I worked in her kitchen."

That terrible night came rushing back, and Caroline closed her eyes, steeling herself against tears as she forced herself to keep telling the story. Opening her eyes, she shared the next part.

"The night before I got here, I was called into Mrs...well, it doesn't matter what her name is. I was called into her office. She told me that her brother needed a wife to gain an inheritance, and as her ward, she was giving me to him. We would be married the following day. We'd be married, and I'd live with him."

"My word," Mrs. Meeks said as she sat back in her chair.

With a deep breath, Caroline continued. "I understood him to be a vile man. One who is coarse and mistreats others. A woman who worked at the school told me so, and was fearful for me. So, with a little help from her, I left. I got a stagecoach ticket for as far away as I could, and still allow myself a little money to live on for a short time, and I ran."

Mrs. Meeks' lips were set into a thin line. "Do you know what the man looks like?" she asked.

"I don't," Caroline admitted. "So, I've been jumping at shadows and strangers each time the stagecoach comes in."

"I don't wonder," Mrs. Meeks said.

Caroline hesitated, then admitted, "I have seen a man several times. Once, I saw him outside of here. I don't know if that's the man or not, but the hairs on my neck seemed to stand up, and my stomach clenched with such fear. It was as though my instincts were trying to tell me something."

"Can you tell me what he looked like?"

Caroline nodded. As she described him, Mrs. Meeks shook her head and a look of concern flashed in her eyes.

Mrs. Meeks was silent a moment after Caroline finished. Her fingers drummed on the table, something Caroline only saw her do when she was deep in thought. Finally, she leaned forward, her eyes serious. "Caroline, I don't think you should go anywhere on your own. Stay with me or the doctor at all times. If this man is all you were told, then he's not going to give up an inheritance because you ran. If he has chosen not to get another bride, he's going to come after you, and take you back to get it, because he doesn't want his pride wounded."

A chill worked its way down Caroline's spine. As much as she wanted to protest, she had the feeling Mrs. Meeks was absolutely correct.

Chapter Fifteen

THAT NIGHT AT DINNER, Caroline decided she was going to tell the doctor about the strange man. Before she had a chance to, Mrs. Meeks spoke with a broad smile on her face.

"I'm planning to make one of my cherry pies for the social this Saturday," she said. Turning to Caroline, she added, "You've never been to one of our town socials, but they are quite wonderful. Jim makes ice cream, we church ladies run the lemonade, there's a cake walk, and we auction off pies."

Edward put his fork down and added wryly, "And then the next day, half the town comes and sees me for bellyaches because they ate too much. So, be ready, Caroline. I'm stocked up on bicarbonate and peppermint leaves, but they'll still come in droves complaining they are near death."

Her mouth filled with chicken pot pie, Caroline tried not to laugh but was unsuccessful, and fell into a coughing fit. Across the table, the doctor's eyes were also filled with mirth.

"It's true," Mrs. Meeks sighed. "Some people just don't know how to control themselves."

"I'll be sure I'm not one of your patients, then," Caroline laughed as she dabbed her mouth. "Tell me about the social."

"The townsfolk get together," Edward explained. "Usually every few months. As the weather is so nice, there will be different foods for sale to picnic with. There's music and...dancing," he stumbled over the word, and shoved a bite in his mouth.

"You know," Mrs. Meeks said, "I'd love to show you everything there, but I'm expected from six to seven at the lemonade. Why, Dr. Mason, why don't you and Caroline go together? You young people would have such a good time together. Caroline, perhaps you can even get our fine doctor to dance. A little exercise would do him good. See how red and winded he is, just eating his dinner?"

Caroline stole a peek at the doctor. His face was red with embarrassment. She was sure hers was too.

"Mrs. Meeks," Edward sighed. "For once I wonder if you'd let me ever ask for something first, before you just suggest it. As a matter of fact, I was going to ask you if you'd like to attend with me, Caroline."

Ducking her head, Caroline nodded as beneath the table her fingers twisted the napkin. "I'd be delighted."

"Wonderful," Mrs. Meeks said. She stood and brought over a small cake from the sideboard. "Now, try this. I was going to make one for the cake walk. What do you think?"

Edward eagerly sliced several pieces and slid one toward each of the women before taking one for himself. He took a large bite and shook his head. "It's dreadful," he half mumbled, his mouth full. "Terrible. Just leave it for me. Don't poison those people!" His fork stabbed another piece.

"Why you," Mrs. Meeks said, but her cheeks were as flushed with pleasure as a young woman. "Caroline?"

"It's wonderful," Caroline marveled. "So light!"

"Terrible, you mean," the doctor corrected her, pointing at Mrs. Meeks with his fork. "If she thinks it's wonderful, the next one won't be for us."

The three laughed, and dinner finished in a comfortable way. Caroline felt happy, part of the household, and realized that she'd not felt that content or welcome for a very long time.

It was only when Caroline settled into bed that evening she realized she'd forgotten to tell the doctor her story. She'd need to do that.

And she only hoped he'd be as understanding about her situation as Mrs. Meeks was.

Chapter Sixteen

"DON'T STAY TOO MUCH longer," Edward said, looking up from the notes he was taking. "Mrs. Meeks will have my head if you don't have enough time to dress before the social."

Caroline laughed. She was leaning overtop of her own set of notes, where she was carefully copying the doctor's records. "I've only a few dresses. I think I'll manage quite quickly to change into a fresh one," she said.

"That's what I like about you," Edward said, meeting her eyes. "You're happy to go as you are. You don't pretend to be something to try and please others. My sister is a year older than me, and she'd beg my parents for a new frock every time there was a social event because she wanted to stand out. Then, the day of the event, she'd spend the whole day throwing dresses and stockings and slippers around the room in panic because she wasn't happy with how she looked."

"My goodness," Caroline laughed. "What a mess that must have been."

"You have no idea," Edward grimaced. "Then...her hair. That was an ordeal in itself. I don't understand. She worked so hard to make herself look pretty, and you, you look beautiful no matter what."

Suddenly, he realized what he said and stiffened. "Apologies. I mean—"

"No apologies," Caroline said, and she held up a finger to stop him. Her eyes twinkled as she teased, "That would mean you take it back, and I won't let you."

With a grin of his own, Edward leaned over his notes again, the pencil scratching across the paper.

Caroline studied what she'd written and compared it to what she'd been copying. At least, she tried to. Her eyes kept flicking toward the doctor. With him busy, she decided to take a moment to admire him.

As he leaned on his desk, long lashes fanned across his cheeks. A short curl from behind his ear tumbled forward, and she longed to run her fingers through his hair. What would it feel like? Would it be as soft as she imagined?

She liked how the doctor kept his face cleanly shaved. When she got close to him, his smell of lightly scented soap and just a hint of the chemicals he used to clean with assaulted her senses in the most delightful way.

Caroline gave a little shiver. She wondered what his skin would feel like. As she imagined, she suddenly frowned.

Why was she thinking this? The doctor was kind to her, nothing more. She was a woman on the run. Getting involved with someone, even just in her imagination, wasn't a good idea.

The doctor's chair scraped across the wooden floor, startling her and he stood. "Let's go," he said. "It's quiet. Everyone's getting ready for the social. If someone needs me, they'll know where I am. Tomorrow will be quite busy, so let's enjoy the free time we have now."

Caroline nodded. She reached for her wrap and walked toward the door. As she opened it, Mrs. Meeks was there.

"Oh! You surprised me," she said to the older woman.

"I'm sorry, my dear," Mrs. Meeks said. Concern filled her face. "I didn't want you left alone."

"Why is that?" the doctor asked, as he slipped his jacket on.

Mrs. Meeks looked between Caroline and the doctor.

Caroline nervously wet her lips. "There's...something I've been meaning to tell you," she said softly.

Edward looked concerned. "Is something wrong?"

"Perhaps," Mrs. Meeks said. "Let's talk on the way."

Caroline nodded. She went outside with the older woman, and they waited as the doctor locked the door. His bag in his hand, the three set off down the sidewalk.

They passed the shops, and once they'd left the crowded buildings, Caroline sighed.

"I'm afraid there's something you should know," she said. "I'm...I'm a runaway, I suppose."

Edward raised his eyebrows. "A runaway?"

"Yes." Caroline hesitated. "You recall I told you I was a ward and attended the school for girls?"

At the doctor's nod, she continued.

"What I neglected to mention is that the night before I arrived, I was called in by the head of the school. She told me she intended to marry me to her brother the following day."

"But she can't," the doctor frowned. "You are of age. She's no right."

"Caroline was threatened," Mrs. Meeks said. "And so she left. But a few days after arriving, she noticed a man. She described him to me as she's seen him several times, though he's never approached her. And my dear, forgive me, I don't mean to be nosy, I don't. But I believe I knew which school for girls you went to. I asked a friend who lived up there if she knew the headmistress' brother. She didn't, personally, but she described him very well."

Edward froze, then resumed his pace. He shook his head slowly, looking from one woman to the next. "Do you mean to tell me that man has followed Caroline here?"

Mrs. Meek's eyes filled with fear and she reached for the girl's hand. "I'm afraid so," she whispered.

Chapter Seventeen

"I HAVE TO LEAVE," Caroline gasped. "I can't let them find me." She walked the last few steps to the garden gate and unlatched it. She whirled toward the house, then stopped. Slowly, she turned. "But I don't want to leave," she said, her voice almost a plea.

"And you shan't," Edward said, striding up next to her. "I'll protect you. We will make sure you are never alone. Not even for a moment."

"I've not seen the man, and according to Mrs. Higglesby, there are no strangers in town right now and no one who matches his description. Perhaps it was a coincidence, but being in a crowd is the safest place for you."

"He may come back." Caroline shivered. "He could have seen I was here, return, and force me to go with him."

"If he does, we will be ready," Edward promised her. "Go inside with Mrs. Meeks. Get dressed for the social. I'm going to let Sheriff Taylor know what's happening. He and his men can keep an eye out on strangers in town. He can alert the stagecoach office and they can help watch as well."

"Good idea," Mrs. Meeks said. She led Caroline toward the house.

"I'll be back soon," the doctor called, and dropped his bag on the porch. He turned, and at a fast walk, soon vanished.

"I don't mean to be so much trouble," Caroline said, twisting her fingers together.

"You aren't," Mrs. Meeks said firmly as she picked up the doctor's bag to carry in. "And the doctor doesn't think so either. Oof. I think he must keep rocks in here," she grumbled as she dropped the bag onto the chair near the door.

Caroline didn't answer, the small joke didn't ease her worry.

"Go get changed," Mrs. Meeks told her. "There's a wonderful evening ahead of you. I just know it. I'm going to be in the kitchen putting the finishing touches on my pie for the auction if you need me."

Caroline nodded. She went to her room and locked the door. Her stomach felt sick from fear. How could she even enjoy the social knowing that man might be out there looking for her?

As she turned, she caught sight of her face in the small mirror. She walked over and peered at her reflection.

"Be strong," she told herself. "You aren't alone. Mrs. Meeks and Edward are here to help you."

The sheriff and his men too, now, she supposed. If the others thought that Mrs. Hardy was acting in an illegal way, then perhaps they were right, and she had nothing to worry about. Why, it could even be that this man she'd seen wasn't looking for her, and Mrs. Hardy knew she was in the wrong and wouldn't come after her. The thought made her feel a little better, and she started to unbutton her dress.

It was time to get ready.

Caroline brushed her hair until it shone and left it loose. She put on a deep gray dress, fresh stockings, and her shoes. She turned, trying to see as much of herself as possible in the small mirror.

There was a tap at the door. "Caroline?"

She opened it, her nerves rising at once, and saw Mrs. Meeks. "Is everything okay?" she asked, concerned.

"Oh, yes, dear. I didn't mean to startle you. But I did want to ask if you were almost ready. The doctor is back and is downstairs. If you are ready, I think he is as well."

Caroline's cheeks heated. "How do I look?" she asked, hesitantly.

Mrs. Meeks gave her a critical look, walking around her before she beamed. "Beautiful!" she declared. "If I had a daughter, I'd hope she was as sweet, kind, and lovely as you."

Caroline reached her hand out and squeezed Mrs. Meeks fingertips. "I'm so glad to know you," she whispered. Tears burned in her eyes from the overwhelm of the day's news, but she refused to let them fall. She'd never give Mrs. Hardy or her brother that satisfaction.

"Let's go," Mrs. Meeks said.

The two moved to the stairs and walked down. The doctor was in the drawing room. Putting aside the newspaper, he stood at the sight of them.

Catching himself staring, he cleared his throat and said, "My goodness. The most beautiful women in the town, and both in the same house."

"It does put you in an awkward spot," Mrs. Meeks said, her eyes twinkling. "How will you choose?"

"Perhaps you ladies would allow me to walk to you both the social?" he asked. "I promised to buy lemonade from you, Mrs. Meeks, and to show Caroline the dance floor, if I recall."

Mrs. Meeks picked up her pie and winked at Caroline. "Now, don't let him back out of that," she warned. "The townsfolk would pay good money to see him dance, and I might have made a wager!"

Caroline gasped as the doctor winced. "Mrs. Meeks! You didn't," she scolded.

"I'll bet she did," Edward groaned as he opened the front door. "Let's go. Can't let you lose the bet. What kind of man would I be?"

With a smug look, Mrs. Meeks cradled her pie and walked through the door.

The three left the house, went through the gate, and Caroline carefully latched it. Edward offered his arms, and Mrs. Meeks took one, giggling like a little girl, while Caroline lightly threaded her arm through the other.

She felt a thrill as they walked so closely, while Mrs. Meeks told a story from a previous bet she'd made, and won, on the doctor. When Caroline laughed at one point and turned to look at him, she caught him staring at her. To her surprise, she found herself giving him a smile, which he returned.

Suddenly, Caroline had the feeling Mrs. Meeks was right. There was a wonderful evening ahead of her.

Chapter Eighteen

As THEY TURNED THE corner and the wide street of Cottonwood Falls opened before them, Caroline gasped. In just a few short hours, the place had transformed.

Colorful red, white, and blue bunting lined shop windows, doorways, and awnings. Wagons were gathered around filled with food, drink, and handmade items for sale. The saloon piano had been carried out, and a man sat on a bench, his fingers plinking at the keys. Two fiddles and a harmonica joined in, creating a catchy, joyous tune that made Caroline want to tap her feet.

"I'm over here," Mrs. Meeks said, pointing toward a large table where women had piles of lemons, a sack of sugar, and a large barrel in front of them. "Stop by in a while," she said, and strode over, calling, "Girls, I'll be right there. Let me just drop my pie off at the auction!"

"Well," the doctor said and turned to Caroline. "What would you like to do first? Are you hungry?"

Caroline looked around. There was so much happening, she wasn't sure where to start. Perhaps supper would be nice. "Yes," she answered. "I am rather hungry, actually."

"Let's amble past the wagons. I smell fried chicken. I wonder what else there is." He pointed to a short distance away. "Everyone in town brings out their tables and chairs, or spreads blankets. There's plenty of seating."

"I've never seen anything like this before," Caroline said. "Everyone in town must be here!"

"They are. And they'll eat, dance, drink, and talk until they near fall asleep," the doctor said with a headshake. "Half will miss church tomorrow, and the preacher will use the same sermon he gives each year, about gluttony and idleness. Of those half who aren't there, a full half of them will be sending for me. I'll need you tomorrow, if you don't mind, even though it's a Sunday."

"Whenever you need me, I'll be there," Caroline promised.

She was done running. She'd done that once. This was where she wanted to be. Sensing Edward looking at her, she met his gaze boldly, her decision made. His fingertips brushed against hers, and he opened his mouth to speak, when someone interrupted.

"Doctor Mason and Miss Watson! Cornbread? Hot biscuits?"

Caroline's stomach growled loudly and Margie Sampson laughed. "I take that as a yes."

"Both please," Dr. Mason said, and handed over a few coins. "Caroline, why don't you get those and find us a place to sit? I'll go get the chicken."

Caroline nodded and waited while Margie bundled the steaming breads into a piece of cloth and handed them over. Accepting, Caroline wandered over to the partially filled tables, chose a spot near the end, and waved at the doctor when she caught sight of him. He joined her, one hand holding a plate heaped with fried chicken, and the other grasping two cups of sweet tea.

"Let me help," Caroline said, jumping up. She took the tea and carried it to their spot.

"Best fried chicken in the world," Edward told her as he sat the plate down. "Just don't tell that to Mrs. Meeks."

Caroline laughed. "I find it amusing how the two of you tease each other," she said. "It's as though you are family."

Edward placed a drumstick on a napkin and slid it toward Caroline, then selected one for himself. As she bit into the crispy skin, he answered. "I'm fond of her. She is an amusing lady with a wonderful sense of humor, something that's needed out here. She reminds me of my gram, who I miss."

Caroline nodded. "She does say the unexpected sometimes, doesn't she?"

With a grin, Edward nodded. "She speaks her mind, that's for sure."

"Could I ask something?" Caroline blurted.

The doctor looked surprised. He set down his chicken and wiped his fingers on a napkin. "That sounds serious," he said, giving her his full attention.

"I've been worried," she admitted. "About...what Mrs. Meeks said earlier." She lowered her voice a little. "You went and talked to the sheriff?"

Edward nodded. "I did. He and his men are keeping a close eye out. The sheriff is a good man. If he or his men see this stranger, they'll let us know and keep an eye on him. You've nothing to worry about. He agrees, what was done isn't legal. You aren't in any wrong whatsoever."

It felt as though a weight had lifted off Caroline. She closed her eyes, leaned back in the chair, and sighed. "That makes me feel better," she confessed. "I've been worried."

"I just wish you had told me sooner," Edward said, looking deeply into her eyes. "I could have helped. I know what it's like to run from something, but I promise I won't let anyone hurt you."

Caroline shook her head. "I'm used to taking care of myself," she said. "I didn't really think about it."

"That should change," Edward said, his voice low. "You shouldn't have to take care of yourself alone. You don't have to anymore, not while I'm here."

Chapter Nineteen

CAROLINE THRILLED AT HIS words. She thought she knew what he meant. The undercurrent was there, but there were so many people around, she didn't want to question him, not even teasingly.

She slid the last biscuit toward him. He broke it half and slid one piece back to her, making sure to brush her fingers.

"How about a dance?" he asked, motioning to other couples dancing on a hastily nailed together platform.

With a critical eye, Caroline asked, "Will it hold?"

Edward laughed, "It usually doesn't break until the end. I will likely treat a few twisted ankles. Now is the best time to go, while it's still sturdy enough."

The small band still played, and Caroline realized her toes had been tapping along, as had the doctor's fingers.

"Well, then. Yes, that sounds wonderful," she said.

They stood and joined the others. "I have to admit," Caroline whispered, leaning in close as he took one of her hands, "I've not danced much with a partner. In school, we only learned the waltz."

"Don't worry," Edward said. "I'm practically an expert. No one will know." He guided her, the two of them bouncing and gliding across the floor. "My mother made me have lessons, and this is similar to a polka," he said. "She wanted me to be able to handle any social situation."

"You are from a well-off family, aren't you?" Caroline asked as they spun.

"Yes. Well, was. Remember, I gave that up."

They turned and whirled.

"What did your parents think when you told them you weren't going to stay there and start a practice?"

He thought for a moment, as he turned them in the opposite direction. "My father was upset. I think time has cooled him. I'd like to reconnect one day. I still write to my mother. But I have never asked for anything from them. My gram, when she passed on, left me an inheritance that my father couldn't control. Gram knew my heart, and my desire to help others. So, I manage that carefully, and use it to supplement my income here. Really, it's quite ample, and if used carefully, should last a long time."

"It sounds like she cared deeply for you," Caroline said, slightly out of breath from their dance. "Is the music getting faster?"

"It is," Edward said. "They'll play faster and faster until the couples drop out."

"I'm nearly there," Caroline admitted.

"Me too," he panted. "But last one standing wins, and Mrs. Meeks has a bet. I can't let her down."

The music kicked into a frenzy, and around them the other couples stopped, some tumbling over from exhaustion. Edward warned, "Hold on to me," and before Caroline could answer, he picked her up around the waist and spun her.

One of the fiddles became screechy, but still they spun and danced as the frantic music set the remaining dancers' pace.

Edward placed Caroline down, never stopping the twirl. The music ended suddenly, and there was a loud burst of applause and cheering.

Slightly dizzy, Caroline looked around in surprise. It looked like the entire town was watching them. They were also the only dancers still standing. She smoothed her hair and tried to catch her breath.

Mrs. Meeks stepped forward. "Pay up, ladies and gentlemen," she said. "You'll find me at the lemonade stand!"

There were good natured groans, and Caroline laughed. "You won her the bet," she said, still struggling for air.

"My honor could do nothing else," Edward said, still panting slightly. "But I am in sore need of a drink. Lemonade to celebrate her victory and ours?"

Caroline nodded and followed him over to where Mrs. Meeks was waving happily at them.

"How much did you win, my good lady?" Edward asked, as he dropped some coins on the counter. Mrs. Meeks pushed them back to him. "On the house," she said. "I just won almost fifty dollars."

Edward shook his head. "I don't know how you do it," he said. "Did everyone in town place a bet?"

Caroline laughed. "Good for you," she said, accepting the sweetly tart drink.

"I knew this dear boy wouldn't let me down," Mrs. Meeks smiled. "He never does."

"I want to hear those stories," Caroline said.

"Another day," the doctor said good naturedly.

Customers approached, and Edward took Caroline's arm and led her away.

"Shall we rest a little?" he asked.

Caroline nodded. They found a grassy spot near the small stream that ran through the town and sat watching the dancers who had recovered and were performing a line dance.

"Thank you for bringing me," Caroline said. "I'm having a wonderful time."

"Can I have your company for the next social?" Edward asked.

Her breath caught in her throat. Did this mean the doctor felt something about her or was he just being polite?

Before Caroline could answer, a man came rushing up. "Doc! Doc! Hurry quick! There's an emergency!"

Chapter Twenty

EDWARD BOLTED UPRIGHT. "WHAT'S the matter?" he asked.

"It's Jim. He just collapsed."

"I don't have my bag," Edward said. "I—"

"I'll get it," Caroline said, already on her feet and moving.

"It's in the house, on that chair near the front door," the doctor said, then ran off toward the crowd.

Caroline did the same, running as quickly as she could. She made it to Mrs. Meek's house quickly, unlatched the gate and burst in the house. Finding the doctor's bag, she set off again, slowed slightly by its weight. Perhaps Mrs. Meeks was right and there were rocks inside.

When she approached, the town was quiet. There was a cluster of people all standing around the doctor and Jim.

"Your bag," she said, setting it next to the doctor. She knelt down. "How can I help?"

"I think it's his heart," the doctor said. "He's very clammy."

Jim was pale, though sweat dotted his forehead and upper lip. His wife watched worriedly, her eyes shining with unshed tears. Mrs. Meeks had an arm around her.

"I'm fine," Jim muttered. "Just too old to dance like I used to. That's what I get, trying to keep up with the likes of you to impress my lady."

"I'll get you dancing again," Edward promised, then looked for Jim's wife. "Let's move him to his bed," Edward said to her. "Caroline, please carry my bag."

"I'm feeling better," Jim said weakly.

"And it's my job to be sure you stay that way," Edward said firmly. "Let me do my job now, so you can do yours later."

Several of the men helped Jim up and carried him to the house above the general store, the doctor leading the way. Caroline followed with the doctor's bag.

The doctor unbuttoned Jim's shirt and listened to his heart with his stethoscope, counting the rhythm. He examined the man's fingernails, his eyes, and listened to his heart again.

"Caroline, please take notes," Edward said.

With a quick nod, Caroline took the small pad of paper and pencil in the doctor's bag and recorded his findings.

The doctor listened to Jim's lungs, counted his breaths, and then reached into his bag.

A short time later, Jim was in his bed, having been given a sleeping draught by the doctor.

Edward spoke quietly to Jim's wife. "Keep him calm, quiet, let him rest. He's a strong man and his heart is sounding good. If you need me, come get me. I'll check on him in the morning."

"That you, Dr. Mason," Mrs. Jefferies said with a watery smile. She tried to press a coin into his hand, but Edward pushed it back at her and shook his head.

Edward and Caroline left, and he took his bag back from her. "Apologies for an interruption to our evening," he said.

"It happens," Caroline said lightly as they exited onto the street. "It was a frequent occurrence in our house."

"I meant to ask you," Edward said, as they rejoined the remaining townsfolk who were still chatting, just quieter now, mindful of Jim in his bed, "I know your father was a doctor. And he also learned medicine up north. What was his name?"

"Charles Watson," Caroline answered.

"Charles Watson. Charles Watson. The name sounds familiar. Though, I can't recall how," Edward muttered.

"In between his trips to help those in the areas far from towns, when he was back home, he also taught at one of the universities. When I was a small girl, sometimes Mama and I would listen to his lectures."

"So, you've always found medicine interesting?" Edward asked.

"I have," she said. "I enjoy helping others, and the reward that comes from that."

"It's definitely needed here," Edward said, nodding at the town. "No matter that these people can't always afford care. They should have it still. We are all the same. Beings who need compassion and assistance."

Caroline rested her fingers on the doctor's arm. "I love that about you," she said quietly, as the times he'd helped others without pay flashed in her mind.

Edward looked at her, and his eyes seemed to pierce through her. "There are a good many things I love about you, Miss Watson."

Chapter Twenty-One

CAROLINE'S HEART THUNDERED IN her ears. The two paused, stopped beneath one of the few trees in town. Her mouth suddenly dry, Caroline realized she wasn't sure what to say. Her experience with romance had been severely limited, up to this point.

Edward leaned closer, and his breath tickled her cheek as he whispered, "Caroline, I—"

"Heading back?" Mrs. Meeks asked as she walked up. "I heard about poor Jim."

Edward straightened, and Caroline wondered if that was just a small flash of irritation on his face. Her knees felt weak. Had Edward been about to tell her he loved her? Had he been about to kiss her? Her words were still frozen in her mouth.

"Yes, some rest is the best thing for him," Edward said. "Would you like me to carry that?" He gestured to the empty pie pan.

"I have it, dear, you have your bag," the older woman said. "Caroline, did you have a good time?"

"Yes, it was wonderful," Caroline said. "Well, except for Jim, of course. I hope he makes a swift recovery."

"I'll check on him in the morning," Edward said, as the three set toward Mrs. Meek's house. "Caroline, could I trouble you to stay at the office, to triage patients as they come while I check on him? There will be some lined up before we get there, there always are the day after a social."

"Of course," Caroline answered.

"I'll go with you," Mrs. Meeks said. "I don't want you alone there, dear."

Caroline nodded, feeling grateful.

The last hint of sun had vanished when they got to the house. Caroline bade the doctor and Mrs. Meeks goodnight and went to her room. As she changed into her nightgown, she couldn't help but smile, still hearing the catchy music play in her mind. She hummed one of the tunes as she brushed her hair.

Yes, other than poor Mr. Jefferies, the evening had been wonderful. She crawled into bed and sighed deeply, recalling the strength of the doctor as he lifted and twirled her around during their dance.

When they were by the tree, when he had said there were many things about her he loved...and leaned closer...Caroline couldn't help but wonder what he might have said or what he might have done when Mrs. Meeks had come. Her mind revisited the moment over and over.

If he had wanted to kiss her, would she have let him?

Yes. Most decidedly, she would have.

Though tired, she couldn't help but replay the evening over and over in her mind, until at last sleep overcame her. That night, her dreams were filled with dancing, her fingers brushing against the doctor's hand, and him whispering that he loved her.

The next morning, Caroline and Mrs. Meeks went to the doctor's office to help patients until he arrived. As the doctor had warned, a steady stream of people entered, with several lined up and waiting as she unlocked the door. Many of them Caroline was able to send away with a small sachet of mint leaves or a twist of sodium bicarbonate. Two others were more critical, and waited for the doctor.

Edward came in about an hour later, and Mrs. Meeks left. After the two patients received care, Edward and Caroline spent the rest of the day treating what seemed to be a line that didn't end. As soon as one person left, two more came in.

Soon, they ran out of peppermint, and were low on sodium bicarbonate. Three ankles had been examined.

"I need to order more medicine to have on hand," Edward said, making a list on a notepad. "As well as more herbs. Is there anything else we are low on? I'll telegraph a friend of mine who can get me things in large quantities and send it to me on the train."

Caroline looked at her own notes. "We could use a few more needles for stitching, some quinine, disinfectant, and surgical thread. Each of those are starting to get low in quantity."

Edward nodded and added the things to his list. Rising quickly, he strode over to the door, looked out, and then called, "Billy! Billy!"

Caroline peered through the window. Across the street, a boy ran over.

"What you need, Doc?"

"Take this to the telegraph office," Edward said, and handed the boy some coins. "Keep what's left. How's your Ma?"

"Better," Billy answered as he looked at the coins. "Thank you, Doc. I'll do it right away!"

Caroline turned as the doctor came in. "I think that's it for the day," he said with a yawn. "I hope so anyway. It feels like we treated about a third of the town."

Caroline nodded, stifling a yawn of her own. She reached for her shawl and draped it over her arm. As the doctor locked the door, her eyes traveled to the stagecoach station, where they were unloading passengers.

A man exited, accompanied this time by a woman. The silhouette was familiar, as was the hat. The woman turned, and Caroline felt sick to her stomach. It took all of her being to wrench herself out of her shock and move. With a sinking dread, she gave a cry of fear and spun around as she grabbed Edward's arm, fearful the woman would turn and recognize her.

"It's Mrs. Hardy!"

Chapter Twenty-Two

Before Caroline could say another word, the doctor had his office door unlocked, opened, and pushed her inside, locking it once they were in there.

"The woman who was your guardian?" he asked, peering through the window.

"Yes," Caroline said. "The man with her is the one I kept seeing here. He really must be her brother."

Edward paced the room. "Stay here," he ordered. "I'm going for the sheriff."

"Don't leave me," Caroline begged, rushing to him. "Please!"

The doctor took her into his arms. "I'll never leave you, Caroline," he promised. "But I must get help. They must be apprehended. It's just two doors down. I'll find the law and a way to get you home safely."

Caroline nodded, her head against his chest. She looked up at him, and the fire in his eyes surprised her.

"When I come back," he said, swallowing hard. "I have something to tell you. Something I've been trying to say for a while."

He pulled her close, and Caroline felt a faint pressure on the top of her head. Was that...a kiss? Before she could wonder, he had released her and moved toward the door.

"Get into the exam room," he ordered. "Stay away from the windows."

With a nod, Caroline dashed toward the exam room, and slid down in a corner. She heard the outer door close and lock.

Her heart was pounding, her hands were shaking. The sick feeling in her stomach returned and she prayed silently, terrified to do anything else.

She hoped Edward would return soon with the sheriff. She also hoped Mrs. Meeks was safe.

Mrs. Meeks! They knew where she had been living, so what of Mrs. Meeks? The older woman was defenseless. And it was likely they'd go to her house. She had to help Mrs. Meeks. She couldn't let anything happen to the woman who had been so kind to her. Even if Mrs. Hardy went there with no intention of violence, who knows what lies she might tell?

That thought fueled Caroline forward. She crept into the outer room, slipped near the window, and looked out.

In the street, everything appeared normal. A chicken wandered down the middle of the road, two women were walking past holding baskets for the market. A wagon was hitched across at one of the stores, the horse's feet shuffling as it waited. Yes, no matter which way she turned her head, it looked clear.

Caroline gave a shiver and moved toward the door. She was terrified to open it, but her desire to help Mrs. Meeks was stronger.

If any harm came to the woman, because of her...

No. She refused to think about that. Edward had gone for the sheriff. She would warn Mrs. Meeks. The woman had done so much for her, she deserved nothing less.

Caroline stood tall, straightening her spine. She slowly, slowly unlatched the door and opened it a crack. Nothing happened. That gave her the confidence she needed and she pulled it wide, her eyes focused on the sidewalk and escape.

Still seeing no one, she eased the office door closed behind her and went as quickly as she could down the sidewalk. She didn't get far when she stepped forward and heard a voice. "There she is," and rough hands grabbed her.

Caroline struggled. She tried to scream, but one hand was wrapped around her mouth, another around her waist.

Chapter
Twenty-Three

CAROLINE FOUGHT WITH ALL she had, but her long skirts hindered her. Tears of anger leaked out of her eyes as she tried, and failed, to regain her freedom.

A wagon pulled up, and she was hoisted into the back, her assailant next to her. Caroline broke away, but before she could scream, she saw a body lying next to her.

"Edward!" she gasped, crawling to him.

The assailant smirked. "He thought he'd go tell the sheriff I was here," he said as the wagon drove at a high speed out of the town. "Caught him right outside the door."

On her knees, Caroline frantically checked the doctor's pulse. He was alive. She sat back on her heels in relief, then slid across the wagon bottom as the wagon took a turn too quickly.

The man in the back gave a mocking bow. His balding head was slick with oil and his shirt, which was too small for him, had a large sweat stain spreading from the neck. An overlarge mustache drooped and he said, "It's so good to finally meet my intended wife."

Caroline watched the landscape whizzing past them. She could jump and try and run, but she'd likely break a bone. And what of Edward? She couldn't leave him. Instead, she straightened her spine as best as she could.

"I am not your anything," she pronounced. "I am of age and have the legal right to make my own decisions."

Mr. Hardy chuckled. "That's cute. We'll see how fast you change your mind once we get you and the good doctor into our hideout."

"Hideout?"

There was no answer to her query, but the wagon slowed. They pulled up alongside an old shack, where a partially falling barn stood.

"Come on," Mr. Hardy growled, and grabbed her arm.

"I'll get her," Mrs. Hardy's tone of disapproval was a verbal slap to Caroline. She turned her head and looked at her guardian.

"Caroline," the woman said, cooling her tone, filling it with one of sorrow. "After all that I have done for you? My dear," she added, putting warmth into her voice, "you know I only want what is best for you. I'm wanting to help you become a member of good society."

Better to play along, instinct told Caroline, and she nodded. "Yes, ma'am," she said, her voice trembling.

Mrs. Hardy smiled and then turned a hard gaze toward her brother. "See? I knew she'd listen to me. Let me handle this."

Her brother grunted and pulled the doctor from the wagon. Caroline winced when Edward's head struck the side. Mr. Hardy dragged him into the barn.

"Careful," Mrs. Hardy scolded. "Do you know how much money his family will give us to return him? He's worth nothing if he dies or he's hurt, you idiot."

A rush of gladness washed over Caroline. They didn't intend to hurt Edward. Mr. Hardy set him down on a pile of straw. Mrs. Hardy walked Caroline in the barn, and to a chair. She pointed at it, and Caroline sat. Mrs. Hardy tied her to the chair with a swiftness and knots so securely Caroline wasn't expecting it.

"My dear, you would have been quite happy as Mr. Hardy's wife," she said. "And, as I am of a generous nature," she paused, and Caroline nodded, lowering her head, "I shall perhaps allow you a chance to return to us. Alive and mostly unharmed. Then you'll appreciate what that means a little more."

Mrs. Hardy removed her lacy handkerchief from her sleeve. Caroline could smell the familiar strong perfume from the short distance.

Buy time. She had to buy time. She didn't know if Edward had alerted the sheriff or not, but she had to give the law the time they needed to find them, just in case.

When Caroline didn't go back to Mrs. Meek's house for dinner, the woman would surely know something was wrong.

Mr. Hardy walked over and squinted at her. "She's sure pretty," he said. "You picked me a good one."

Mrs. Hardy rolled her eyes. She shoved the handkerchief into Caroline's mouth. "We'll talk more later," she said. "I am returning to town to get some food." With a warning glance at her brother, she added, "Stay and watch them."

"Yes, sis," Mr. Hardy said, and sat on a stool a few feet away. He pulled out a pocket knife and began to clean his fingernails.

As Mrs. Hardy walked away, Caroline looked over at the doctor. Edward still hadn't moved. She closed her eyes and prayed.

Dear God, please, let the sheriff find us. Keep Edward safe.

Chapter
Twenty-Four

IT WAS HOT. IN the barn, there was no air movement and the old, musty smelling hay made it hard to breathe. Caroline could tell she wasn't alone in her discomfort. Mr. Hardy's face was red and sweat dropped off his face. It was disgusting.

She glanced again at Edward. He had twitched slightly. Her eyes darted to Mr. Hardy, who was mopping his face with his stained handkerchief.

Looking again at Edward, she saw his eyes were open. She gave a tiny shake of her head, hoping he would understand. He gave a small nod and closed them again.

Good. Better they think he was hurt or asleep. That might let him regain his strength enough to help free her.

Unless...

Caroline wiggled. She knew it wouldn't do anything, but she was trying to get Mr. Hardy's attention.

"Mmmphhh?" she mumbled around the soggy cloth in her mouth.

Mr. Hardy looked up from the ladle of water he was drinking. "What?"

Caroline tried again. "Mmttr?"

With a dull look on his face, he shrugged. "I can't understand you." He took another drink, then straightened. "Oh. Water? You want some water?"

Caroline nodded, putting a pleading look on her face. She fluttered her eyelashes and tried to look demure. Mr. Hardy stepped over with the bucket.

"It is hot," he agreed, and removed her gag. "Don't scream," he warned. "Not that it will do you any good out here, but I don't want to hear it."

As her parched mouth greedily gulped the water he held to her lips, Caroline gave a small nod. When the ladle was empty, Mr. Hardy offered, "More?"

"Please," Caroline said. She forced herself to meet his eyes. "I'd be so grateful, Mr. Hardy."

"Marvin," Mr. Hardy said, as he held the water.

Caroline drank, then repeated, "Marvin?"

"That's my name. With you about to be my wife, I expect you ought to use it."

"Yes, of course," Caroline said. She gave him a faint smile. "Marvin is a very nice name."

Mr. Hardy returned to his stool, but he left her ungagged. Caroline wondered if he was bored. He looked eager to talk to her.

"Why did you run away?" he asked. "Didn't my sister tell you how much money we'd get?"

With wide eyes, and a small shake of her head, Caroline answered, "Why, no, not really. She told me you were due for an inheritance, stipulated by being married."

"That's right. Two hundred thousand dollars."

Caroline gasped. She'd never imagined an amount that large. No wonder Mrs. Hardy was so determined to find her. But...that begged the question, why her? She decided to ask.

"But why did it need to be me? When I left, why didn't you simply find someone else to marry?"

Mr. Hardy snorted. "That was my question. But she didn't like to be outwitted. You made her upset. So, we had to find you, bring you back, and remind you who was in charge."

Caroline nodded slowly. "And, the doctor?" she asked.

"We knew you were working for him. He might have known about us, so we watched the both of you. Sis found out he's from a wealthy family, so figured if the opportunity came, we could ransom him." Mr. Hardy chuckled, "A bride and a dowry. Not a bad day's work."

Caroline wondered if she should say anything else. Perhaps tell them Edward was estranged from his family?

But if she did, they might not find a reason to keep him alive or unharmed. She pulled at the rope knots on her wrists. Her hands ached.

Mr. Hardy's eyes followed her movement. "Nope," he said. "Not letting you loose. I'll keep the gag out though."

"Thank you," Caroline said.

They sat in silence. Mr. Hardy kept his eyes trained on Caroline, who kept hers trained on her lap, unwilling to meet his beady eyes.

A short while later, the sound of a wagon was heard. Caroline looked up, hope rising in her chest. Had they been found?

Chapter Twenty-Five

THE BRIEF FLASH OF hope departed as soon as she heard Mrs. Hardy's voice. "Marvin, help carry this," the headmistress ordered from outside the barn.

Obediently, Mr. Hardy rose. A moment later, he returned with his sister, holding a basket.

Mrs. Hardy eyed Caroline. "Are those knots holding?" she asked.

"Yes, ma'am," Caroline answered.

Leaning over, Mrs. Hardy checked them. "Good." She turned to her brother and showed him a scrap of paper. "I brought some bread and cheese and apples. We can eat, then we will leave. We'll head two towns over in the wagon. Here are the directions to get there. Early tomorrow, we can get the stagecoach back home."

"Why not get it here?" Marvin asked. "Wouldn't that be more convenient?"

Mrs. Hardy closed her eyes in a heaven-help-me expression. "Because we don't want anyone to see us with the doctor," she explained, as if she were talking to a child. "That would raise too many questions."

Mr. Hardy nodded and went to the basket. "Let's get packed," he said. "We can eat on the way. Save time."

"I agree," Mrs. Hardy said. The two left the barn.

As their footsteps faded away, Caroline whispered, "Edward? Edward?"

"I'm awake," the doctor said, sitting up. "Caroline, I don't like your choice in intendeds."

Caroline sputtered, nearly choking on her gasp of horror. "He is not my—" and then she smiled as she realized she was being teased. "I'd much rather have someone else," she said, with a tease of her own.

Edward grinned. He sprang up and pulled his pocketknife out, cutting partially through the ropes that held her.

"Enough so that you can break free, but not enough so it looks like you are loose if they come back suddenly," he said. "I'm going to take a look. Wait here."

Edward slid over to the barn door. He took a quick look, then came back. "No good. They are at the wagon." He sat back down. "We'll have to wait a little longer, then run."

Caroline nodded. "Please tell me, did you see the sheriff?"

"No." Edward shook his head. "But I left a note. And when they grabbed me, I dropped my doctor's bag.

Someone will see that, and know it's not natural, and look for the sheriff."

"But how will they find us?" Caroline asked.

"They had to have been seen," Edward assured her. "Their intention isn't to hurt us. We are too valuable to them. It will be alright. I'll get us out of here."

The doctor paused, then sighed. "I should have stayed with you. If I'd stayed, this wouldn't have happened."

"No," Caroline admitted, "It was my fault. I didn't listen to you. I was worried about Mrs. Meeks, so I unlocked the door."

They were quiet. Caroline's guilt for not staying put pressed against her chest, making it hard to breathe. By the frustrated look on Edward's face, she wondered if he felt the same.

Edward checked through a crack in the barn and returned. "Mr. Hardy is still there at the wagon. The man packs a punch. He's so large, I'm not even sure if the two of us could slow him."

Caroline nodded. She remembered those thick, hairy arms around her and how Marvin Hardy had pinned her, lifting her as if she weighed nothing. "We wait," she said.

Footsteps sounded, and Mrs. Hardy walked in. "Good, you're awake," she said as she saw the doctor. She pointed to the ladder leading to the loft. "Stand there."

Edward nodded and moved slowly, feigning a limp. Caroline watched anxiously. What would happen?

Mrs. Hardy followed with a length of rope. She tied his hands to the ladder.

"We'll be leaving soon," she told Caroline, as she tugged on the knots. "Just us three. I will wire a note from the next town to the doctor's parents, letting them know I'll trade his location in exchange for a small sum."

"You can't!" Caroline gasped. "What if they don't answer?"

Mrs. Hardy shrugged. "Then they don't."

"Sis, we got a problem," Mr. Hardy said, stopping at the barn door.

With an irritated expression, Mrs. Hardy turned to her brother. "What is it?"

"Wheel on the wagon is broke. We can't go anywhere."

Chapter Twenty-Six

THANK YOU, GOD. CAROLINE felt a surge of relief as Mrs. Hardy left the barn. She'd never been so happy to hear a wagon had a broken wheel.

Mrs. Hardy returned a short time later. "We'll be staying the night here," she said, irritation evident in her tone. "I'll let you keep the gag out of your mouth, but I'll be watching and listening for any trouble. I advise you, Caroline, to think carefully and make good decisions on whatever actions you take."

Without another word, she spun and turned. Caroline could hear her talking to her brother, though she couldn't make out their muffled conversation. A short time later, there were the sounds of a horse trotting away.

"Gone to get another wagon," Edward whispered, being closer to the door to hear. "He's taken one of the horses. One's left."

Caroline nodded. That made sense. It was obvious none of them knew how to fix the broken wheel.

"Caroline," Edward said. "Now is when we need to go. Our chance is better with him gone."

Her body grew tense. Edward was right, but she was worried. Would the two of them be able to find their way back to town? She had certainly never been to this place before.

"Listen carefully," Edward said softly. "I need you to get loose. Then cut me free. My pocket knife is in my front pocket. Once I'm free, I'll slip out and grab the other horse. He's hitched nearby."

Caroline nodded, listening carefully.

"I'll lead him to the backside of the barn. You come out that door. We'll get on, and go as far and as fast as we can."

"Can you find your way back to town?" Caroline asked.

"I can," Edward answered confidently. "I've been out here before. But we have to hurry. It's starting to get dark. If they think Mr. Hardy can get to town and back with a wagon before it's too dark to drive, we can't be far away. However, the longer we wait, the more dangerous it is, both with his return and the dark."

Caroline peeked outside. Edward was right. She closed her eyes for a moment. In her mind's eye, she saw the scene she'd tried hard to forget over the years. The idea of riding a wagon or a horse at night brought it back to her.

Papa was reading aloud, and she and Mama were rolling bandages. It was after their evening meal, and getting late. The sky was near dark. It had been a gloomy day, and a terrible storm had come through. Caroline had been fearful the small house they were staying in would blow away.

Wind shook the frame, while rain pelted the windows. A small pot was hastily shoved under a leak in the roof. When the storm passed, she'd been grateful. Mama hadn't said it, but she was too.

A knock came at the door, and Papa looked up. He set his reading glasses down and opened the door. It was a young man, begging for help. There had been a fire. Lightning had struck their barn. His ma had collapsed, trying to help get the animals out.

With a nod, Papa gathered his bag and went out to hitch the horses to their wagon. Caroline helped Mama fill a basket with linens, bandages, and salves. They rushed out, closed the door behind them, and climbed in the wagon, with Caroline in the back.

The man raced ahead on his horse. Papa followed in the wagon. It was getting dark, and their small lantern didn't really provide enough light on the rough road.

Suddenly, there was another bolt of lightning. It struck a tree ahead and scared the horse, who bolted. Papa tried to control it, but the wagon swayed side to side and the reins were jerked out of his hands.

In the back, Caroline clung to the sides, trying to keep from pitching out. Suddenly, the wagon stopped with a terrible jolt as they hit a fallen tree laying across the road.

Papa and Mama were thrown from the wagon. The man on the horse had wheeled around and raced toward them.

Everything seemed to move so slowly. Somehow, the wagon was still upright. Caroline struggled to gain her footing and climbed down. The lantern from their wagon lay on its side. A small fire spread from it.

Caroline grabbed the lantern, righted it, and stamped out the fire. In the faint glow, she saw the man leaning over two still forms.

She held the lantern up and moved closer to see better.

"Papa? Mama?"

Chapter Twenty-Seven

"Caroline?"

The doctor's voice cut through her memory. Caroline realized tears were falling down her cheeks.

"Caroline. Speak to me. Are you hurt?"

With a shaky breath, Caroline shook her head. "No. I'm sorry. It's just...riding a horse. At night. Or a wagon. It's...it's how my parents died."

She worked to free herself from the ropes and cleared her throat. With a deep breath, she said, "But we can't help that. We have to go. And I know it. I just remembered. And..." she stopped. What was there to say?

Edward's face was full of sympathy. She moved closer to him and hesitated.

"Where did you say the knife is?"

"My pocket," he said. "In my...trousers."

Her face flamed as her fingers hesitated. The indecency of putting her fingers near such an intimate part made her freeze. What if...

"Caroline," the doctor's voice drew her eyes to his. "Just reach in and grab it. We have to hurry."

Looking away, Caroline reached her hand into his pocket. She slipped her fingers lower until she touched the hard metal knife and pulled it free. It was warm from being so close to him, and her eyes refused to leave the knife as she sawed at the knots around his wrist.

A moment later, and the doctor was free. He took the knife from her and held it in a defensive way as he slid toward the door.

"Meet me at the back," he whispered.

Caroline nodded. She moved to the other door and peered out. "It's clear here," she whispered, as her eyes scanned the forest.

Edward nodded, and crept out of the barn. Caroline rushed to the other side and watched through a crack in the weathered boards. Edward stayed in the shadows, his back against the barn. He was close to the horse, and she hoped it wouldn't snort and give them away.

The house was close by, but the door was closed. Mrs. Hardy must not be concerned about them escaping. Likely it had never crossed her mind they could. Had it not been for Edward's pocket knife, they'd still be trapped in her secure knots.

As Edward reached the horse, Caroline made her way back to the other side of the barn to wait for him.

The horse came a moment later, Edward already on it. He held out his hand and pulled Caroline up behind him. She wrapped her arms around his middle and held tightly.

"We're going to go slow, and quietly," Edward whispered. "Once we get to the road, I'll give the horse his head. He'll help us get back. I know this horse. He was stolen a few days ago from a farmer."

Caroline nodded, her head pressed to the doctor's back. Her eyes sought the sky. It was a dark blue. Not much longer it would be impossible to see the road.

They moved at a brisk walk to keep the horse quiet, but the house and the barn were still too close. Caroline kept watch. She heard a shout from behind them at the same time Edward did.

"GITUP!" Edward hissed, and kicked the horse into a gallop.

The horse broke into a run. Caroline risked a look back, and saw Mrs. Hardy running toward them, holding something in her hand and waving it at them. She couldn't see what it was.

The horse turned sharply as Edward controlled the reins. Caroline clung to him, the sudden swaying reminding her of the terrifying wagon ride.

"It's too dark," she gasped, unable to see the road. "We have to slow."

"A little farther," Edward said, his voice grim. "We have to go a little farther. Then we'll get off the main road, so we don't run into Mr. Hardy."

Caroline didn't answer. She couldn't. Her throat was tight, and anything she might have wanted to say was firmly trapped in it. She was terrified to be riding in the dim light, and scared what they might encounter on the road.

They rode too fast for her comfort, and then Edward stopped, suddenly wheeling the horse around.

"Someone's coming," he whispered. He led the horse into the woods. Trees would provide cover, though not entirely, but with the dim light, it would make them harder to see against the thicker trunks.

They dismounted and crouched near a thick shrub. It provided good cover, but would it be good enough? The horse was still visible. Edward looked at it, shook his head and looped the reins over the horse's neck. He gave it a smack on its flank, and the horse set off.

Caroline's mouth became dry as the rider came closer. There was the familiar rattle of a wagon. There was only one person who it could be. Mr. Hardy returning.

Chapter
Twenty-Eight

As she closed her eyes, Caroline just knew the thudding of her heart could be heard over the rattle, rattle, creak of the wagon as it came past.

Crouched beside her, Edward's hand rested reassuringly on her arm, as the two held as still as they could. Caroline's eyes opened, but all she could see was the brush in front of her.

Her lungs ached from the breath she was holding, scared that any tiny movement would give them away. She was sure Edward felt the same, as when her eyes darted to him, he was staring with an intense look of concentration and small beads of moisture had formed on his brow.

The wagon slowed. Caroline tried to hold in her gasp, but it released. Luckily, the wagon's driver and passenger didn't notice, and it set off again.

Caroline waited, counting to one hundred before she let out her breath and relaxed.

"Gone," Edward whispered. "It was him. But we need to stay low." He took her by her hand. "Let's go this way. The wagon can't follow us. There are too many trees and shrubs. We'll be able to have some cover."

With a nod, Caroline followed him, and the two picked their way carefully through the dimming forest. Though they tried to be as quiet as they could, there was no way to entirely avoid the loud snapping and cracking of twigs and small branches that broke underfoot, or the swishing and rustling of fallen foliage as they moved over it.

Caroline tripped once, her foot dropping into a small hole in the ground. Luckily, Edward was nearby and steadied her.

Not long after, Edward stopped and cleared his throat. Caroline looked at him, puzzled. "Is something wrong?" she asked.

"Ah," Edward flushed slightly, and released her hand to scrub it over his face. "It would appear that we are going around in circles."

Caroline turned, surveying the areas. Was he right? She wasn't sure. With a small shrug and a little laugh, she admitted, "I wasn't paying attention. I was just following you."

"Well," the doctor said, with a sheepish grin, "I admit, I am not the best navigator. I was counting on the horse to get us most of the way. With the shadows rising, it's a little harder to pick out the landmarks I am looking for."

"Should we stop for a while?" Caroline asked. "I don't really want to be here in the woods all night, but it's getting dark. We don't have any light, and it's going to be impossible to find our way back to town."

"I think we had better," Edward admitted, after he turned a slow circle. "It's getting too dark but once the sun is out, it won't be hard at all to find the road and head back to town." He pointed to a wide tree down in a small valley. "Let's go there. It will provide cover on one side, it's low enough that anyone crossing above might not see us below, and the trunk is thick so we can rest against it."

The doctor stepped down the small hill and offered his hand. As she took it, Caroline used her other to raise her skirt enough to not trip. A moment later, the two reached the tree, and not a moment too soon. It was now so dark Caroline could hardly see her hand in front of her face.

"No moon tonight, I guess," she whispered.

"Luckily," Edward said. "We don't need it telling them where we are."

They sat in silence for a few minutes.

"I'm sorry," Caroline said, interrupting the stillness. "This is all my fault, and I apologize."

Edward's voice sounded incredulous. "It's not your fault at all. You had nothing to do with us being kidnapped, nor our being in the woods. However, you did help us escape."

"Not without your help," Caroline answered. "We make a good team."

"We do, don't we?" Edward said.

Caroline heard a rustling, and Edward's fingers found hers. In the dark, she allowed her shy smile as the warmth from his hand calmed her nerves.

"I've been thinking," Edward started.

"About what?" Caroline asked.

"This whole thing has made me realize something. You know, I wasn't completely honest, either. Coming out west to treat others wasn't the only reason I came."

Caroline waited, her curiosity growing.

"You see, there was a girl back home. Since we were children, our parents planned that we would marry. The only problem was, she was too much like a sister to me. We were friends. That's it. I wasn't interested."

"So, you left in part because of her?" Caroline asked.

"Yes. I supposed you could say I was running away from an arranged marriage too, though not to the extent you are."

Caroline smiled, even though she knew the doctor couldn't see. Humor laced her voice as she teased, "I'd have never guessed you'd run from anything."

"It was more of knowing what I wanted, and that wasn't it," he replied. Then, in a serious tone, he added, "And just like I knew I wanted to treat anyone who needed medical care, whether or not they could pay for it, there's another thing I know."

"What's that?" Caroline felt the doctor squeeze her hand gently before he answered.

"That I don't want to be without you. Caroline Watson. I'm in love with you and I want you to marry me."

Chapter
Twenty-Nine

A SHOCK RAN THROUGH Caroline's body at his words. He...loved her? Her chest was tight, not from fear, but from overwhelm. From unknowing what to say or do.

Edward continued, "Before you say anything, I wanted you to know you don't have to feel the same. You don't even have to say yes. We can keep things the same if you want. I just...after today, I knew it. And I wanted to tell you." He snorted, "And I wanted to do it before Mrs. Meeks put the words in my mouth. That old busybody."

The tension that had filled her broke at once, as a laugh bubbled up inside and burst through Caroline's lips. "She might have, I could see it," she giggled.

The doctor raised Caroline's hand, and a moment later she felt the brush of his lips against the back of her hand. "Dare I hope," he asked, "that you feel the same?"

Caroline felt lightheaded at his question. Did she? She was glad it was dark. She wasn't sure how she looked right now, but it was likely quite a fright. Her hair was a half-tumbled down mess and her dress stained and dirty. It wasn't exactly a romantic setting for a declaration of affection, and yet, she wasn't sure she'd have it any other way.

"Ah, if you want to answer... I mean, I know I said you didn't have to, but I didn't really mean that." Edward's wry tone broke her thoughts.

"Forgive me," Caroline said. "I was just thinking."

"What about?" The tension in his voice was unmistakable.

"About how I look dreadful. We are out in the woods, being chased by two kidnappers. One who wants me for their wife, and the other who wants to ransom you."

"It is quite a story, isn't it?" Edward chuckled.

"Yes, and one I would very much like to tell at our wedding," Caroline answered.

"At our..."

Caroline felt Edward sit up, his grip around her hand tightening. "Does that mean—"

"Yes," Caroline breathed, moving closer to him. "Yes, I love you too, Edward Mason. And I don't want to be without you, either."

Caroline wished then she could see him better. She felt the warm breath from Edward's lips as he moved closer and brushed his mouth against hers. He pulled back just as suddenly, and she felt him drop her hands.

"Edward?"

"One moment," he answered. "I'm just looking for, ah, yes, I found it." There was the rustling of paper. "Give me your hand."

Caroline obeyed, and held it out, moving till she bumped him in the darkness. "What is it?" she asked.

"I don't have a ring yet," he said. "But I have something I hope you will like just the same, until I can get you one."

She felt the paper press into her hand. "A piece of paper?" she asked.

"After you told me your father's name, all night I thought about where I'd heard it. Then, I remembered. About fifteen years ago, he'd written a research paper on the properties of the Jimson Weed. My professor made me read it, form my own opinion after some further research, and write a paper on it as well."

"I don't understand," Caroline said.

"It was the last published paper by your father," Edward explained. "And it went directly to the university. They are the only ones with a copy of it. Well, until now."

Caroline clutched the paper to her chest. "Do you mean this is a copy of his paper?"

"Yes," Edward said, and the pleased expression in his voice told her he understood just how much this meant to her.

"There are others coming too. My gift to you. Anything that Charles Watson wrote, I have a friend finding and collecting for you. We can get it bound into a volume."

Her throat felt thick with emotion, and a tear slid down her cheek. "This means more to me than you could possibly know," Caroline whispered. She closed her eyes and pressed the paper to her heart.

"Do you accept this then?" Edward asked. "In lieu of an engagement ring until we get back to town and I can order one, proper like?"

"Oh yes," Caroline laughed, her heart bursting with joy.

She moved closer to Edward and rested her head on his shoulder. A chill had filled the night, and she shivered. She wasn't sure if it was from happiness or the cold, but she knew without a doubt Edward loved her, she loved him, and if they could just find their way back to town, Mrs. Meeks would be overjoyed at their news. She only wished she had more family to share her joy with.

As those thoughts swirled in her mind, Edward put his arm around her shoulders. Her eyes growing heavy with exhaustion, and her body chilled from the night air, Caroline closed them for just one moment, leaning into his warmth...and opened them again as someone shouted, "Doc!"

Chapter Thirty

"It's the Doc and Caroline," a man shouted. "Get me a blanket. She looks froze through."

Caroline sat up and looked. She couldn't see anyone. It was morning though, and the brief closing of her eyes must actually have been hours. Edward was standing, and waving his arm. "Sherriff! You found us!"

"The sheriff?" Caroline struggled to stand. Her dress tangled in a shrub's branch and snagged, tearing. She sighed as she looked down. There wasn't going to be any way to save her dress.

Edward took her arm and pulled her up the slope. A warm blanket was wrapped around her and a wagon pulled up a moment later, Mrs. Meeks in the passenger seat.

"Oh, my dear girl," the older woman said as she threw herself at Caroline.

The two embraced. As they did, Caroline saw she still held her father's paper. Relief washed over her.

"We caught them, heading toward the train station," Sheriff Taylor was telling Edward. "We were going to take them in for questioning, when I spotted a note I'd given you in the wagon's back. As soon as I asked where you were, the two of them turned on each other quick. Got the whole story out of them. Good thinking on your part to drop that in before you took the horse."

"And then the sheriff came to tell me," Mrs. Meeks said. "Of course, I wasn't going to stay home and worry when I could be searching." She took Caroline's hand. "You must be so tired and hungry," she said. "Let's go back. I'll make us a fine meal."

"I'd be so grateful," Caroline said. "I could use something warm."

Edward helped her into the wagon seat, then Mrs. Meeks, and climbed in the back. "Do you need us to give a statement?" he asked the sheriff.

"I will," the man agreed. "But you two get some rest and food, and get cleaned up. I'll come by tomorrow. That's plenty of time enough."

Caroline frowned, her eyes filled with worry. "What if they get out?"

The sheriff shook his head. "No chance of that, Miss Watson. The U.S. Marshals are here guarding them. Turns out, Mr. Hardy is wanted in quite a few places. His sister, too."

"I declare," Mrs. Meeks said, with a shake of her white head, "what a story this will be to share later."

With a shy smile, Caroline said, "I've got one to tell you too," she said.

With a sharp expression, Mrs. Meeks glanced from Caroline to the doctor, and a slow smile formed as the horses walked forward.

Chapter Thirty-One

CAROLINE TURNED, TRYING TO see every bit of herself in the tiny mirror. Giving up, she sighed and began to pace. Behind her, Mrs. Meeks clucked.

"You look lovely, dear," she scolded, as she tugged on Caroline's pale pink dress.

The two had worked on Caroline's wedding dress for nearly a month, sewing every spare moment they had. A decorative row of ivory ribbon bows went down the front, and small gathers along the side were also decorated with a bow. Small, satin covered buttons rose up her back.

"Now relax, before you wear a hole in my floor." Mrs. Meeks picked up the small, slightly oval hat trimmed in velvet and lace Caroline was planning to wear and eyed it critically, as she arranged the small white flowers on it.

"I'm sorry," Caroline said, with another, deeper sigh. "I'm just so nervous!"

"What on earth for?" Mrs. Meeks asked. "It's all working out beautifully. You and the doctor are getting married this afternoon, you'll still be living here with me, that horrible woman and her brother are behind bars, and it's a beautiful day. You've nothing to fret about."

Caroline nodded, and picked up the hat, placed it on her head, and peered into the mirror. There was a knock at her door, and she turned.

"I wonder who that is?" she mused and reached for the handle. As she opened the door, she gasped at the sight of the person behind it.

"Mary!"

"Caroline!"

The two women held each other tightly. Caroline's eyes pricked with tears.

Mary held her at an arm's length and shook her head. "My goodness, aren't you a vision," she said. "So beautiful! When I got your letter, I could hardly believe all you said in it. I had to read it several times."

"A lot has happened," Caroline admitted. She squeezed her friend's hands. "I'm so glad you are here! But why didn't you tell me you were coming?"

Mary laughed. "It was faster to just come," she said. She walked in the room and extended her hand. "Mrs. Meeks? Caroline told me all about you."

"And she's told me all about you," the older woman said warmly, ignoring the offered hand and hugging the cook instead. "We are so delighted to have you here. You must stay with us while you are in town."

"I'd appreciate it," Mary said. "With Mrs. Hardy being locked up, the school is shut down."

Caroline's hands flew to her mouth. "Oh no! What will you do?" she asked.

Mary shook her head. "I don't know yet, but I'll figure out something."

Mrs. Meeks put her arm around the woman, and said, "Caroline says you are quite wonderful in the kitchen. You know, now that she and the doctor are getting married, I have an extra bedroom, if you'd like to stay on. In town, the hotel is needing some help. I'll put in a word for you," she said.

"That would be wonderful, and I'd be obliged to you, ma'am," Mary said happily.

"Nonsense. Making matches is what I do best," Mrs. Meeks said. Then, she leaned forward, and with a wink whispered, "They always work out."

Caroline overheard and laughed. "They really do, Mary."

***

"IT'S TIME," MRS. MEEKS said, a short while later, and Caroline walked down the stairs and out into the garden where the entire town was gathered. She held a simple bouquet made up of several of Mrs. Meeks' fall flowers.

The saloon piano had been brought over, and one of the church ladies played soft music as she drew closer.

There, among the beautiful garden, her friends, and the people of the town she'd grown to love, the pastor married Dr. Edward Mason and Caroline Watson. They shook hands afterward and gave embraces as the townsfolk gave them gifts.

Tables were heaped up with pies, both sweet and savory, biscuits, cornbread, apple cider and tea, and everyone ate until they were near bursting.

Caroline and Edward traded grins at the head of a table, and he raised a glass to her. "Mrs. Mason," he said. "I have one last gift for you."

"You don't need to give me anything else," Caroline said. "I have you."

Edward shook his head. "I want to give you this." He reached into his waistcoat and handed her an envelope.

"Is it another paper of Papa's?" she asked as she eagerly took it.

"No," Edward said. "Did you know your father had a brother?"

Caroline looked at him, surprised. "No, I didn't."

"Well, he did," Edward said. "You've a whole other family you never knew about. And one day we're going to meet them."

"I'd like that very much," Caroline said. "I look forward to meeting your family as well."

"My parents are most eager," Edward assured her. "I wrote them and had a telegram sharing their excitement. My father and I have set aside our differences. One day soon we will travel north for you to meet them. I know they will love you as much as I do."

Caroline's heart was bursting with happiness. She had everything she could want. She had two wonderful friends, the right to make her own choices, more opportunities were opening for women in the medical field, a handsome man who loved her, and now, a new family. Was there anything else she could ask for?

Edward met her eyes and reached for her hand.

No, Caroline thought. There's nothing more I could possibly want.

All of her worries and fears left her the moment Edward Mason had asked her to marry him. Caroline knew that she'd spend the rest of her life by his side, and together they'd make a difference to all those they served, especially to each other.

As a fiddle began to play, another joined in, followed by a harmonica. Edward stood. "May I have this dance?" he asked, giving her a small bow.

"Five dollars that the doctor doesn't stop dancing till dark!" Mrs. Meeks shouted.

"I'll take that bet!" Jim Jefferies called back. "I say he stops in an hour."

"Two hours!" another voice called.

Edward groaned, rolled his eyes, and Caroline reached for his hand. "Can't let her down," she laughed.

"I love you," Edward said, staring deeply into Caroline's eyes.

"I love you," she answered.

Other couples joined in the lively dance, and together they spun around and around the garden.

Cottonwood Fall, Kansas. The place where dreams come true.

Epilogue

CAROLINE SAT AT HER desk, a thick book in front of her. As she turned a page, she stopped to scribble a note.

Edward came from the back room, three-year-old Lizzie following him, a bandage in her chubby hands as she tried to imitate her father wrapping it. He leaned against the doorframe and patiently showed her again. The toddler copied the movements, then yawned and rubbed her eyes.

"I'll take her home to Mrs. Meeks and start my rounds," Edward said, scooping Lizzie up, and walking over to Caroline. He gave her a kiss and left the office.

Alone, Caroline bent her head back over the notes. The new information that had recently been discovered about the weakness of lungs and a possible treatment by an herb was fascinating. She wanted to copy the information that had been sent to them from Boston.

There was the sound of someone coming up the wooden sidewalk and she looked up as the door opened.

Carley Madison stood there, a nervous expression on her face. The fourteen-year-old was the daughter of the postmaster and his wife, who had come to Cottonwood Falls about two years prior. She was a quiet girl, but one with sharp eyes that took in everything she saw.

"Hello, Carley. How can I help you?" Caroline asked, as she observed the girl's fingers nervously smoothing, and smoothing again, her skirts.

"Dr. Mason, I'd...I'd like to learn medicine from you. Will you teach me?"

About the Author

Sarah Lamb is the mother of two boys and wife to a teacher. She spends her days writing and editing books in the beautiful Shenandoah Valley. Sarah loves nothing more than high-quality books that both entertain and open the reader's mind, allowing them to dream, and then later make those dreams come to life.

Could I ask for one small favor? Reviews like yours on Amazon mean so much to me and help others to find my books! Thank you for supporting indie authors!

Stop by my website to see everything I've written and keep up to date!

www.sarahlambbooks.com

More Books by Sarah Lamb

Want more of Sarah's books? She writes for children and adults! Find them all on Amazon!

Fiction for Adults

Caroline (Runaway Brides of the West Series)
The Christmas Treasure (Holiday Cottage Series)
Mathilda (Rescue Me: Mail-order Brides Series)
Louise (Rescue Me: Mail-order Brides Series)

Fiction for Children

Morgan and the Fey
Thought is Not the Boss of Me
Bubble Gum Wishes (Coming soon)
Equaleria's Daughter (Coming soon)
Plug and Play (Coming Soon)
The Eighth Door (Coming soon)

Non-fiction

How to Manage Food Allergies at Disney World and Other Important Vacation Planning Tips to Save Money and Have Fun, Not Stress

How to Advocate For Your Child's Needs (Coming soon)

How to Vacation with Food Allergies (Coming soon)

Want to keep running away?

With over twenty books in this amazing Runaway Brides of the West Series, you can run (and find true love) forever! Check them all out on Amazon today!